**THEY HAD SPENT A FULL DAY CAMPING.
THEY LOOKED FORWARD TO A GOOD NIGHT'S
SLEEP . . .**

Then suddenly from behind the lean-to, off toward Eagle Ledge, came a heart-stopping scream—not a howl, not a wail, but a scream, unlike any sound either boy had ever heard before. It was a horrifying, insane sound that gripped the boys with fear.

"What was that!" Seth whispered.

"I don't know."

Both boys lay frozen in their sleeping bags, too afraid to blink. . . .

Bantam Skylark Books of Related Interest
Ask you bookseller for the books you have missed

ALVIN FERNALD: TV ANCHORMAN
  by Clifford B. Hicks

BANANA TWIST by Florence Parry Heide

BIG RED by Jim Kjelgaard

BOB FULTON'S TERRIFIC TIME MACHINE
  by Jerome Beatty, Jr.

BONES ON BLACK SPRUCE MOUNTAIN
  by David Budbill

C.L.U.T.Z. by Marilyn Z. Wilkes

DON'T STAND IN THE SOUP by Jovial Bob Stine

THE FALLEN SPACEMAN by Lee Harding

THE INCREDIBLE JOURNEY by Sheila Burnford

SNOWSHOE TREK TO OTTER RIVER by David Budbill

THE WACKY WORLD OF ALVIN FERNALD
  by Clifford B. Hicks

WILD TREK by Jim Kjelgaard

David Budbill

BONES ON BLACK SPRUCE MOUNTAIN

A BANTAM SKYLARK BOOK®
TORONTO • NEW YORK • LONDON • SYDNEY • AUCKLAND

RL 5, 008–012

BONES ON BLACK SPRUCE MOUNTAIN
*A Bantam Book / published by arrangement with
Dial Books for Young Readers*

PRINTING HISTORY
Dial edition published May 1978
Bantam Skylark edition / February 1984

*Skylark Books is a registered trademark of Bantam Books, Inc.
Registered in U.S. Patent and Trademark Office and elsewhere.*

ISBN 0-553-15234-3

Published simultaneously in the United States and Canada

PRINTED IN THE UNITED STATES OF AMERICA

O   0 9 8 7 6 5 4 3 2

For Frank and Eva,
keepers of the mountain

BONES ON
BLACK SPRUCE MOUNTAIN

1

"Do you think they'll let us do it?" Daniel questioned.

"I don't know," Seth replied. "Let's do it anyway. Just take off."

"They'd think we ran away. They'd send a search party."

"So what. We could hide. If they came looking for us they'd get lost."

"We wouldn't?"

"You want to back out? I think you're scared."

"I am not! I want to make this trip as much as you do."

"Well, if you get cold feet sitting in your own dooryard, what are you going to be like up there on the mountain?"

Seth and Daniel lay stretched out under the huge pine tree in Daniel's dooryard staring at the mountains in front of them. They liked looking at the mountains and especially at *the* mountain, Black Spruce Mountain. Four miles away as the crow flies, it stood above its neighbors like a huge fist thrust against the sky. Just now the bare rock cliff on its western face shone darkly in the afternoon sun.

Ever since the boys had been friends, they had watched the mountain together. It was more than just a mountain to them. They couldn't say exactly what it represented but it was important. Ravens nested there; bears lived in the cracks and caves; the big deer, the wise ones, the ones hunters never shot, wandered there. Coyotes howled from its upper ridges, and even though no one had ever seen one, there were still stories that up there, somewhere near the top, a panther prowled the night. It was a place for no man, not to mention two thirteen-year-old boys. Yet, in an odd way, the mountain drew the boys to it. It was as if the mountain had a voice, as if it sang to them, calling them out and away from the safety and comfort of their homes, away from the ordered brightness of their daily lives and into the murky dangers of a mystery. The mountain was a wild and strange place, a place for dark creatures and marvelous adventures.

"You think I can't take it up there?" Daniel asked. "You can't be serious. I know as much about the woods as you do, maybe more."

"You do not. I've lived around here all my life."

"What's that got to do with anything? Just because I haven't been around here since I was a baby doesn't mean a thing."

"Well, I can take care of myself."

"So can I. I know what it's like out there too. I know a hell of a lot more about how to survive than you do."

"Big man. Come off it, Daniel. Besides, nothing's going to happen we can't handle."

"I'm not saying it will. All I'm saying is, we better not get too cocky about this thing or we might end up being sorry."

"Okay. We won't."

"I just don't want to run away, that's all. Taking off like that is no good. You don't know what it's like."

"You do?"

Daniel stared at the ground. "I . . . ah, forget it."

It was late in August. Summer was almost gone. On the far hills the boys could see here and there a poplar or a soft maple turning yellow, red. Cries of insects filled the air. It was a frantic, intense sound, heard only at the end of summer, in those few weeks before the first killing frost. The green world was giving way. Soon the trees would stretch their skinny fingers against the sky. Fall, that cold invader, stood waiting impatiently on the other side of the mountains.

Seth and Daniel knew they were like the insects; their summer lives were coming to an end. Two weeks from now, every morning, they would leave their hill farms and travel down the mountain to Judevine, the village in the valley below. School again. Their days of freedom were almost over.

"Go ahead," Seth said. "What were you going to say?"

"Nothing."

"Daniel, you always do that! You're always starting out on something and then stopping, like I wouldn't understand. What is it?"

"Nothing. I don't want to talk about it. Look, let's not fight. It's just our folks have got to know; we've got to ask them. I'm not going unless we do."

"Okay! Okay! We'll ask."

From where they lay, the boys could see off to their

right the upper end of Bear Swamp. The great blue heron who lived there moved about more now. He too knew the time to leave was coming. They could see the brook winding through the middle of the swamp. In their mind's eye they could see the trout, the ones they hadn't caught, finning quietly in the shadows. To their left the dirt road that passed in front of them slipped down into a small ravine, then climbed a hill and disappeared around a bend toward Seth's house and farm a mile farther up the road. In front of them, beyond the barn and meadow, the woods began. From there as far as the two boys could see, there was nothing but trees and mountains. They were surrounded by trees; in fact, both Seth's and Daniel's farms were little more than small open places in a forest that seemed to stretch endlessly away in every direction.

"Daniel, we've just got to make this trip; we've got to climb Black Spruce. I want to know what's up there; I've always wanted to know, ever since I can remember."

"We'll go. It's important to me too."

"Okay, then."

"I think we ought to give ourselves a week, five days at least," Daniel continued. "It's a long way up there and there's no point in getting all the way up and having to turn right around and come back. We could start getting our stuff together in the morning, take off the next day."

"Good," Seth said. "I'm going home. I'll ask Dad. No, Mom. No, Dad would probably be best. Tonight, before chores. You do the same. Come up to my house after breakfast and we'll start packing. That is if . . ."

"Don't worry. They'll say yes."

By the time Seth reached home, supper was on the table. Halfway through the meal he could contain himself no longer. He couldn't wait to find his father alone. Besides, it might be better if he asked them both at once. "Ah, Daniel and I want to go camping in the mountains, okay?"

"Not so fast," his father said. "Where do you want to go?"

"We thought we'd go up Tamarack Brook to Raven Hill and make a camp up near Morey's old sugarhouse, where I was last fall. Then we could explore Lost Boy Brook ravine from there and climb around on Eagle Ledge and Black Spruce. We'd be gone about five days."

"I don't know," his father said. "That's a long time to be away. It sounds like risky business to me."

"It does to me too," his mother said, "but he spent the night alone in the swamp last fall and that went all right. He works around the farm like an adult now; he's getting older. I'm worried too, but I think we should let them do it."

"Well, I suppose. But I don't like it much."

Seth wanted to shout, but he didn't. All he could think about was what was happening a mile down the road.

The next morning as Seth and his parents sat eating breakfast, Daniel came running up the lane. He burst into the house panting like a dog. The smile on his reddened face said it all. Seth's mother laughed. "Well, I guess that settles it."

His father wasn't laughing, only smiling a kind of halfhearted smile. "I suppose it does."

"Come on, Daniel, let's go into the living room."

Seth spread the topographical map out on the living room floor.

"We could take off from your house," Seth said. "We can work our way up the Tamarack, up through here, and fish as we go. Then we can camp near Morey's sugarhouse the first night."

"Maybe we shouldn't spend time fishing until we get our camp built," Daniel said. "We don't know exactly how long it'll take us to get to the sugarhouse. It looks like it's about four miles from my place. That's

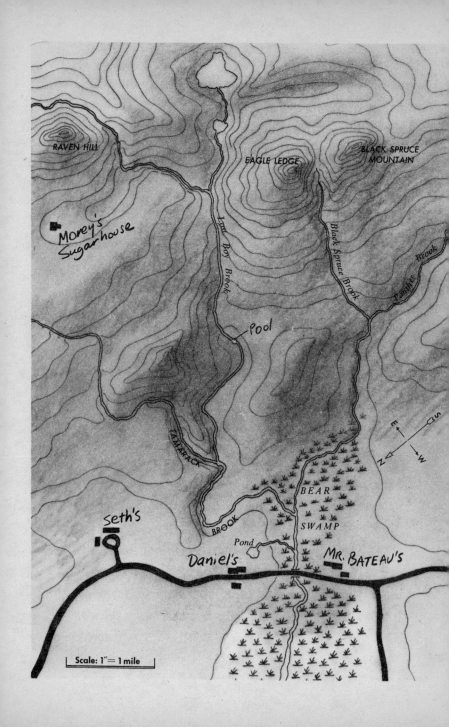

a pretty good walk for one morning through that kind of country with our packs. If we could get there in time for lunch, we'd have the afternoon to fish and get the camp built."

"You're right," Seth said. "We probably shouldn't fish on the way up. It took me a long time to get up there last fall. Hey, maybe we won't have to build a camp the first day. Maybe we can spend the first night in the sugarhouse. There's a shed off the back; I saw it last fall. There's even a bunk and a stove in it. I bet if we cleaned it up a little, it would make a good camp. We could dump our stuff and go down to Lost Boy Brook and catch our dinner."

"Good idea. Then the next day we could fish, lie around and stuff, and get ready for our climb to Eagle Ledge and Black Spruce."

"Yeah." Seth lowered his voice so his parents couldn't hear. "Maybe we could climb down the cliff on Black Spruce. Let's take some rope." Then his voice grew louder again. "When we got back, we could spend another night or two in camp and come home. Four or five days. That's what I told Dad."

With that settled, the boys began to get their equipment together. They tried to divide the weight evenly between the two packs.

SETH'S PACK

sleeping bag
6-by-8-foot plastic tarp
nested cookpots, including:
  one 2-quart pot
  one 8-inch fry pan
  one coffee pot with lid
  two 7-inch plates
  two plastic cups
  one pot lifter
cooking grill
fishing rod and reel
canvas creel
hooks, sinkers, flies, worms
whetstone
toothbrush
roll of toilet paper
food, including:
  whole potatoes
  rice
  dried shell beans
  salt pork
  two onions
  bacon
  sugar
  salt and pepper
  chocolate
  one dozen eggs
  pancake flour
  tea
  mixed nuts and raisins
  peanut butter
  powdered milk
extra clothing

DANIEL'S PACK

sleeping bag
small folding shovel
cruising ax
folding saw
fishing rod and reel
canvas creel
small bag of fishing tackle
map and compass
50 feet of stout rope
baler twine
small bag of nails and tacks
toothbrush
cold-water soap
fly dope
four candles
flashlight
first-aid kit, including:
  gauze pads, adhesive
  bandages, safety pins,
  two ammonia inhalants,
  scissors, tweezers, burn
  ointment, roll of adhesive
  tape, aspirin, roll of gauze
  bandage
extra clothing, including:
  two pair of socks
  one cotton shirt
  one pair of underpants
  one T-shirt
  one bandana
  one heavy wool shirt
  needle and thread, some
  buttons

Each pack weighed about twenty-five pounds, easy to carry across a room, but another matter entirely to carry miles and miles up a mountain.

Early the next morning Seth and his parents arrived at Daniel's house. As the boys prepared to leave, their parents stood chatting nervously, trying not to show the concern they felt. Old man Bateau was in the kitchen too.

Mr. Bateau was the next neighbor down the road. He lived alone. Almost every morning he came by to pay a call and gossip. The boys liked Mr. Bateau. He was the oldest man on the hill and full of stories about the wilderness. Until his wife died, Mr. Bateau had milked cows like the rest of the farmers on the hill, but he was never what you could call a farmer, not the way Seth's and Daniel's fathers were. Old man Bateau never really cared for cows. He was first and always a woodsman, a logger. He was always the first man into the woods in the spring to cut next year's firewood. He was never really happy unless he smelled of sweat and pitch. Mr. Bateau was seventy-five now, but he could still work a day in the woods as well as any man. It seemed to the boys he knew more about the woods and the animals than any person alive.

He had taught them everything they knew about

camping. He was the one who showed them how to make a lean-to out of poles and boughs, how to start a fire with yellow birch bark, how to build a fire pit so that food would cook slowly and not burn. He had been a good teacher.

When he heard the boys were making a trip, the old man's eyes sparkled. He seemed almost more excited than they were. The boys knew somehow that only old man Bateau understood how much they wanted to go to the mountain.

"So. You babies go to da woods, eh?" Mr. Bateau often called the boys babies. Had anyone else in the whole world referred to them that way they would have been fighting mad, but coming from Mr. Bateau it was okay. They understood; in fact, they liked it. "I wish I go too. You little fawns be careful. Da woods is good. Dey make you grow, 'cause you see strange t'ing der. You see fear. Dat good for you. But you be careful! Da woods don't care for you da way your mudder and your fadder do. Dey soon as see you die up der as come back. Da woods don't hurt you, but dey don't he'p you neider. You mus' be smart in da woods, not dumb like a cow. Da woods dey stronger dan you little babies. Watch like a deer, den you be okay.

"You boys go to da mountain too, no? Yes. I

know. I go der once too, long time ago. You boys go look for da bones, too. I know, I know. Da bones no good! Stay away from da bones! Dat little baby lost and starve to death in dat cave, poor little t'ing, he didn't have no chance up der. He see da fear and he go crazy; dey heard him cryin' in da night. Stay away from da bones! My fadder seen 'em once when he was young and dey turn his hair white as January. He see da fear too, only he be lucky; he come back. Babies, you do what I ask you; don't go near da bones!"

There it was again. Seth and Daniel had heard the story of the bones on Black Spruce Mountain a thousand times it seemed. Every kid in Judevine knew the story.

Seventy-five years before, in Hardwick, the town on the other side of the mountains, there was an orphan boy whose foster father beat him mercilessly. The boy ran away one day, off into the mountains, and was never seen again. Although search parties were formed and the mountains combed thoroughly, not a trace of the boy was ever found. Years later someone, nobody knows exactly who, found the skeleton of a boy in a cave on the western face of Black Spruce Mountain. The bones lie there to this day, or so the story went. Some people said that since the boy was never properly buried, his ghost haunted the mountain.

For a few years after the boy's disappearance, during haying, always during haying, people could hear howling, or maybe it was crying, from the mountain. Everyone agreed there was a strange sound up there, but they couldn't agree what made the sound. Some said it was just bears howling the way they sometimes do in the summer. Others claimed it was young coyotes. Others said it was proof there was still a panther up there. Still others said it proved that the spirit of the boy really did haunt the mountain.

Mr. Bateau's version of the story said that the boy didn't die right away, but rather that he learned to survive and lived up there in the cave for years. Mr. Bateau claimed that the cries people heard weren't made by a ghost at all but by the boy himself and that the cries were cries of loneliness.

For a few years after the boy disappeared, strange things happened on Mr. Bateau's farm. At that time Mr. Bateau's family lived on Daniel's place. The first year, in the fall, some canning jars of vegetables and meat disappeared from the cellar, and a couple of horse blankets and an old pair of woolen pants disappeared from the barn. The Bateaus were never sure that the things were actually stolen; maybe they were just misplaced, but it was strange nonetheless. Then the second year no food or clothing disappeared, but a shovel and a hoe came up missing. After that, for a few years nothing very unusual happened, but occasionally a part of an old machine or a piece of scrap metal or a small can of nails would be gone. Then nothing, no strange cries from the mountain, no little thefts, nothing.

Slowly, over the years, people forgot the details of the story. Slowly the tale took on the sound of something from a book. Everybody more or less forgot—everybody, that is, except Mr. Bateau.

When Seth and Daniel were younger, they were frightened by the story and believed it. Now that they were older, they realized that grown-ups told the story because it was a good yarn, but they knew nobody really believed it. Seth and Daniel didn't really believe it either.

Nobody believed the story except the little kids and Mr. Bateau, and Mr. Bateau was old and a little peculiar. At least that's what people said. Nobody alive had ever seen the bones. Old man Bateau's father was the last man said to have seen them and he'd been dead for years. And since nobody went up to the mountain, nobody even knew whether there really was a cave on the western face. Anyway, it

23[

would be impossible for anyone to survive up there. It was just a story, a story for little kids and old men who were kind of crazy. But though the boys doubted the story, it still fascinated them. The possibility that it might be true added excitement and mystery to their plan.

By the time Mr. Bateau had finished talking, the boys were ready. They mounted their packs, kissed their parents good-bye, and headed down the lane toward the meadow behind the barn.

"You boys be careful!" Daniel's mother shouted.

"We will!"

The five adults stood in the dooryard and watched the boys grow smaller as they moved across the meadow toward the woods. Then the long early-morning shadow of Black Spruce Mountain fell on them and took them in.

In the batting of an eye they were gone, swallowed by the woods, and there was nothing left to look at but the mountain reaching darkly into the sky.

2

Seth and Daniel struck the old logging road that ran alongside Tamarack Brook and headed upstream. It was a warm, clear day and the cool shade of the woods felt good. Already their pace had slowed from the fast, striding eagerness with which hikes always begin to a slower, steadier gait, the sure sign of those who know that there are many hard miles ahead.

"Daniel, do you think Mr. Bateau really believes that story?"

"Nah, how could he?"

"I don't know, but when he tells it, it sounds so real. And he sounds so sincere."

"I know."

"Maybe he's right," Seth went on. "He was right about the beaver pond and the big trout in the middle of the swamp. Nobody believed that story either until we showed them proof. I hope he *is* right. If we could find the bones, we could prove to everybody he was right about that too."

"Well, I don't believe the story. Look, Seth, have you ever seen or heard a ghost? All that stuff can be explained. Can you imagine a kid surviving up there for years? It's impossible. He'd freeze to death the first winter. What would he eat? How would he stay warm? It's impossible. All of it's impossible and you know it. Why would a kid do such a thing anyway? There's nothing to that story and there never was."

"Maybe not, but it'll be fun to look for the bones even if we don't find anything." Seth was determined not to let Daniel spoil the adventure.

The logging road hooked left and back toward the farm. Seth and Daniel dropped down over the bank of the brook and began hopping from rock to rock, working their way slowly upstream. Their rubber-bottom, leather-top boots were perfect for terrain such as this, not as hot as all-rubber boots, yet water-proof enough to travel through brooks and swamps. Ahead of them the boys could hear the dull roar of a waterfall. The ravine narrowed as they approached until, when they stood at the bottom of the falls, the sheer rock sides rose almost perpendicular far above them. They would either have to climb hand over hand up the ravine walls or retrace their steps and find a way around. Slowly they inched their way up the falls, gaining one plateau after another, with great effort and even greater care, until they stood panting at the top. Their hearts were pounding now, not so much from the exertion of the climb as from the fright they felt on looking back down to where they had been.

The boys let their packs down slowly and settled themselves on a flat jut of rock about the size of a kitchen table. They rested briefly, listened to the roar of the falls, then headed upstream again.

They came to a place where another old logging road crossed the brook. The log bridge had long since collapsed and been washed away.

"Hey," Seth said, "I know this place. I was here last fall. This road will take us to the sugarhouse."

The woods were remarkably still that morning. Only an occasional bluejay squawked away in front of them, announcing their presence to the unseen creatures all around. They followed the slight two-track depression of the ancient woods road up a gentle rise and through a flat, mature stand of hardwood trees. The August sun made jigsaw patterns of light and dark as it danced across the forest floor.

Although Seth had been here before, things looked different now. The trees were still in leaf; the ground was choked with ferns and bushes. Seth couldn't be quite sure they were going in the right direction. But every now and then he saw a tree or a certain clump of trees or a wet place or a rock that gave off a familiar feeling. Although he didn't know exactly where he was, he wasn't lost either. He moved forward now, not with the kind of knowledge one gets from a map, the kind the mind deliberately retains, but rather with that strange sense, those vague feelings of what is right and wrong, stored in him from last fall's hike, feelings he hadn't known were there until now. It was the instinctive knowledge that he had been here before.

They came to a fork in the road. Seth picked the direction that felt best and they pushed on. Seth knew his chances of finding the way were good if he could keep himself from doubting his feelings. If he could trust that odd urge to go this way instead of that, he'd get them there, but it was hard to do. Ever since he'd started school, he'd been taught to think, not feel, taught to mistrust his instincts. It was hard now to go forward riding entirely on a kind of knowledge he'd been told to disregard—hard but not impossible, and before long the angular lines of Isaiah Morey's sugarhouse loomed in front of them.

The boys dropped their packs at the gaping open side of the ruined building and stepped in. Everything was the same as it had been the year before, the same litter of beams and gnarled tin, the same broken table and chair, the same ladder made from poles leaning against the wall. There was one change, however. The porcupine Seth had found stiffened and bloated with death, was now deflated and shrinking to a small clot of rotting hide and bone.

Seth stepped around the porcupine and gingerly opened the door that led into the sugarhouse shed. During the winter the shed roof had caved in from the weight of snow, and now the shed was filled with a rubble of rafters and metal roofing. Where Seth had found an old and dirty but useful place to stay, he now found a chaotic tangle of decay. The shed would be useless as a camp. The boys would have to make other plans.

The collapsed roof had allowed light and rain to

come in, and weeds were growing in the shed. The old coat Seth had found last fall hanging from a nail on the wall had fallen to the floor, where it lay limp and wet. There were raspberries sprouting from the soggy mattress on the cot. The place wasn't a shed anymore; it had become a confused pile of sticks and tin. Last fall Seth had felt the presence of the men and women who worked here years before; now he felt nothing. All the ghosts were gone. The place was too far gone even for them. There was nothing left, only the last remains, only that final sinking back into the earth. The shed was slowly returning to the ground. The boys stepped out into the sun.

"Now what?" Seth asked. "We can't stay in there. I wouldn't want to if we could."

"Well, for starters," Daniel replied, "how about some lunch? I'm starved."

"Good idea. There's a nice big beech tree right up over the bank. I had lunch there last fall. Let's go up there."

The boys settled under the beech and ate sandwiches and apples.

"We better not hang around here too long," Daniel said. "We don't have a camp; we don't have any fish. We've got a lot of work to do before dark and it must be noon already. Let's slide down into the ravine and work our way upstream until we find a good campsite. If that doesn't take too long, we can probably get set up before dark."

The boys headed down a long sidehill covered with young spruce and fir not more than three feet high. The whole hill had been logged over a few years before and the young trees were growing profusely in the bright emptiness left by the loggers. Once into Lost Boy Brook ravine, however, huge ancient trees covered up the sky again.

They stopped here and there on their upward climb to debate the merits of this spot or that as a campsite. They needed easy access to water. The brook would supply that. They also needed a level place on which to build their lean-to. Here in the lower reaches of the ravine the banks were far too steep. They continued up the ravine. Finally, far up into the mountains they found a spot where a small brook joined the main stream. Near the angle made by the junction of the two streams, there was a large, flat place clear of underbrush in a stand of tall hemlock and spruce. This was obviously the place. They unpacked. Seth put the folding saw together and looked around for poles with which to begin building the camp. He turned to see what Daniel was doing. Daniel had his fishing rod under his arm and was tying a hook on his line.

"What are you doing?" Seth demanded.

"I'm going fishing."

"Fishing? We've got a camp to build. It's the middle of the afternoon. You're the one who rushed us over here to get to work."

"Well, you build. I'll fish."

"Come on! We can eat beans and bacon if we have to. Put away the fishing tackle and let's get to work."

"It's not that big a job. We don't have to do everything together all the time. I'll help you when I get back. Up here I ought to be able to get a dozen in half an hour. I won't be gone long."

"No sir, mister man, you're not going. I'm not your slave you know. You're going to help me here."

Seth dropped the saw and grabbed at Daniel's fishing rod. Daniel pushed Seth away hard, knocking him down. As Seth got up, he saw Daniel's right hand ball into a fist, his knuckles whiten.

Seth took a step backward. "What's the matter with you!"

Daniel's hand loosened. "I don't know."

There was a silence in which both boys stood shaking, looking at each other.

"I'm sorry, Seth. I don't know what got into me. I'll stay here. We'll work on the lean-to together, then if we get done in time we can both go fishing."

The two boys began gathering poles for the lean-to, but the incident had taken away the pleasure they usually felt in working together. Usually they got along well. Now something was different, something was wrong.

Seth and Daniel had been good friends since the day Daniel was adopted by his parents five years before. There had been arguments, of course, and even an occasional fight, but never anything serious—except once. A couple of years ago, they had gotten into a fight, a real fistfight. Seth had given Daniel a bloody nose and Daniel had cut Seth's lip badly. But as soon as there was blood, the fight had stopped. Both boys were ashamed. Their feelings had been hurt more than their faces. They wanted to be friends; they *were* friends. They had vowed to each other never to do it again. A fight was not exciting the way it seemed on television, but ugly and brutal, something that made them feel bad about themselves. And yet all that afternoon it seemed Daniel was ready to break their vow, ready to fight again.

Seth knew there were times when Daniel became so angry that he nearly lost control of himself; he'd seen it happen at school. But usually Daniel tried to hold back his anger; in fact, most of the time it seemed to Seth that Daniel was too controlled, too withdrawn and cool. But now Daniel's anger had risen into his throat. Seth could hear it in his voice. Seth felt that at any moment Daniel might explode, and it frightened him.

Maybe Daniel was upset because their plans had gone awry. Maybe it was being so far from home, so totally alone in the wilderness. Or maybe it was something else, something Seth couldn't understand. Whatever it was, it bothered him. They had so looked forward to this trip, and now that they were actually doing it, it wasn't any fun. The bad feelings made everything difficult, and building the lean-to, something both boys always enjoyed, now loomed ahead of them like a chore. But like all chores, it had to be done.

The boys were lucky enough to find two spruce trees close enough together that they could nail the crossbar to each tree about four feet above the ground. Then they placed the foundation logs, about four inches in diameter, on the ground to make a six-by-eight-foot rectangle. With baler twine they lashed the pole rafters to the crossbar so that they slanted downward to the back where the boys nailed them to the head log. They set small poles close together along the sides of the lean-to and trimmed them at the roof line. Later they would weave balsam fir and hemlock boughs between the upright poles to make sidewalls.

All the wood used for framing was dead wood. The boys didn't want to cut any more live trees than they absolutely had to. Now, however, they did need to cut one live hemlock, about a foot in diameter. They sawed the butt log into four-foot sections to serve as reflector logs for the back of the fire. The hemlock boughs would make the weaving material for the side-walls and bedding for the floor of the lean-to. No part of the tree would go to waste; they would use it all.

As the boys broke the soft, fragrant hemlock boughs away from their branches and laid them carefully layer upon layer on the lean-to floor, Mr. Bateau's words of instruction echoed in their minds: "Break little! Break little! You want to sleep on da boughs of da hemlock tree, not on da tree!"

Doing the things Mr. Bateau had taught them, hearing his gentle instructions in their heads, made the boys feel better. It seemed as though Mr. Bateau were there with them, and his presence, even if it was only in their imaginations, made them feel more comfortable, more secure.

With the soft, springy, deliciously sweet bed of hemlock complete, the boys tacked their tarp over the rafters and then covered it with branches to keep it from flapping in the wind.

They wove the boughs into the sidewalls and the lean-to was complete. There would be time later for the little refinements, the cozy touches, that would make the lean-to a homey place to spend time. It looked good; Mr. Bateau would have been proud of them.

The lean-to had taken a long time and most of the afternoon was gone. The boys really should have turned immediately to the construction of the fireplace and cooking range, but since they both were feeling better now and wanted to try some fishing, they agreed they could get along without it for one meal. They got their fishing gear together and headed upstream to find some trout.

The fishing was better than their wildest dreams. Far up here in the mountains the trout had never even seen a hook before, and they lashed out voraciously each time a worm tumbled down the current toward them. Seth and Daniel soon discovered that although the trout hit hard, they were wild and very wary of any strange shadow across the water. If the boys accidentally approached a likely-looking hole with the sun at their backs so that their shadows reached the brook before they did, there would be no action in that place; it would seem as if there were no trout there. It wasn't long before they learned always to approach a hole with the sun in their faces and to keep low. These trout had to be stalked. The new method of fishing was exciting. It was more like hunting than fishing, and the results were magnificent.

Quickly their creels filled with small but fat brook trout with the dark, almost black bellies that are so often the sign of high, wild mountain trout.

As the boys worked their way slowly upstream, the crystal-clear, glacial-blue brook water gradually began to darken. Now there were fewer and fewer cleanly washed stones, more and more rocks covered with a dark green moss. Both boys had seen this happen to a brook before. It always meant still water ahead. And the only thing that still water meant was a pond, and in a place like this only beavers made ponds. As the boys pushed forward, they could see on both sides of the brook that telltale beaver sign, pointed stumps sharpened like pencils. They clambered over the tangle of sticks and twigs that was the dam and found themselves looking across a small beaver pond that stretched out in front of them through a maze of drowned trees.

"Wow! Look at that!" Seth said.

"Yeah, that thing must be full of trout. I bet nobody has ever fished it. Let's give it a try."

"I think we should get back to camp," Seth said.

"It's going to be dark soon and we've got to cook supper. It'll be here in the morning. Besides we've got more than enough to eat."

"Go ahead back. I'm staying."

"Come on, Daniel. It's suppertime."

"Cook it yourself!"

There it was again, Daniel's anger, welling up apparently out of nowhere.

"Okay! Be pigheaded!" Seth shouted. "I'm going back, but don't think I'll have supper ready for you when you get there. You can fix your own damn supper!"

Seth stomped off down the brook. Daniel stood on top of the beaver dam and watched Seth disappear.

As Seth poked his way back to camp, he wondered what was eating at Daniel. At times like this Seth felt that he didn't know Daniel at all, that Daniel was a complete stranger.

It wasn't long after Seth arrived at camp that Daniel showed up.

"Did you get anything?" Seth asked.

"Nah, I didn't even fish it. I followed you right back down. Seth, I'm sorry about up there."

"It's okay."

"You don't sound like you mean it."

"I don't. What's wrong with you?"

"I don't want to talk about it."

"There you go again! You're always saying that! You've been meaner than a she-bear all afternoon and all you can say is you don't want to talk about it. How can we ever be friends?"

"What do you mean? We're friends."

"I don't know, Daniel. I don't think we really are. What's wrong with you?"

Daniel turned his back to Seth and said nothing.

"Okay, don't answer! I don't care anyway."

"Look, Seth, can't we just forget it?"

"No."

The boys began fixing a supper of bacon, trout, potatoes, and tea. They really didn't need the bacon, but they needed grease for cooking in the days to come. It was hard cooking without the proper fire pit and cooking range, but they managed. They ate their meal mechanically, both of them too preoccupied to enjoy themselves.

Finally Seth gathered his courage again and said, "Daniel, are you nervous?"

"Nervous about what?"

"I don't know. Just nervous."

"Nah."

"Well, something's wrong. I haven't seen you like you were this afternoon since that first fall in school.

Remember what a fighter you were? You were some mean dude!"

Seth smiled as he said it. It was an amusing, almost fond memory for him.

Daniel wasn't smiling. His eyes were glassy, far away. "I remember" was all he said.

"Maybe I *am* a little nervous," Daniel continued. "But I don't know what about. I just don't feel right. Maybe I'm getting sick."

"Do you think it's the boy?"

"Are you kidding? I told you I didn't believe that stuff and I don't. I don't even think about that story. That's not what's bothering me. Let's not talk about it anymore."

3

After the boys finished supper and washed the dishes, there was just enough dusky evening light left to construct the reflector logs for the back of the fire. They cut the butt log from the hemlock tree into four-foot sections and stacked them one on top of the other to a height of about three feet. Hemlock was the best wood for a reflector because it didn't burn easily; it tended to char over and go out. They positioned the back logs about five feet in front of the opening to the lean-to and drove stakes into the ground behind the reflector to support what amounted to a log wall behind the fire. The reflector logs were very important. Heat and light bounced off them back into the cooking utensils so that food cooked more evenly. But even more important, the back logs reflected heat and light into the lean-to, creating a warm, bright room in which the boys could laze away the dark hours before they went to sleep.

Daniel had gathered some yellow birch logs for the after-dinner fire. No nighttime campfire was complete without the delicious smell of yellow birch smoke. Yellow birch smoke smelled just like . . . like . . . yellow birch smoke. For Seth and Daniel that distinctive odor was as much a part of the woods as the woods themselves.

Now with the sweet smoke lacing the air, the boys hunkered down on the foot log of the lean-to and commenced the serious evening business of staring at the fire.

"Got your pipe?" Daniel asked.

"Yup. You?"

"Yup. Where did you get the tobacco?"

"The usual place," Seth said with a smile unseen in the darkness.

Both boys filled their pipes and began to smoke. Neither really smoked, not like some of the kids at school who had cigarettes with them all the time. They'd tried cigarettes and disliked them; they'd even chewed tobacco a couple of times, just as their fathers did, but neither one of those habits had ever stuck. In fact, the only time they ever smoked was while they were camping, at times like this. Maybe it was because Mr. Bateau smoked a pipe only when he was working or camping in the woods.

The night was quiet, the fire warm. Only an occasional crackle or spurt interrupted the perfect stillness all around them. It was like old times. Daniel felt better. He relaxed, his anger gone as if it had been carried away by the smoke that climbed high into the night sky. Now he wanted to talk.

"Okay," Daniel said, "I admit it. I *am* nervous or something, at least I was this afternoon. Maybe I do think about that story more than I'd like to admit. But I still don't think we'll find any bones. It's just a story."

"That's right," Seth agreed, "but it's hard to get what Mr. Bateau said out of your head. Say he's right. Say we do find the bones. What difference does it make? There aren't any ghosts or anything. Bones are just bones, right?"

"I guess so." Daniel puffed on his pipe, paused a moment, and then said, "Look, this is ridiculous. We're too old for this stuff. There's only one way to settle this thing."

"Tomorrow?"

"Nah. I'm in no hurry. Are you?"

"Nah."

"Besides, we haven't done any real fishing yet. What say we finish getting the camp in shape after breakfast, then pack lunch and spend the rest of the day fishing that beaver pond we found. We could climb Black Spruce day after tomorrow."

"Sounds good to me," Seth said. "Let's get some sleep."

Both boys stepped around behind the lean-to to urinate before turning in.

"You know," Daniel said, "when I was a little kid I could pee about ten times this far. I remember, years ago, when I lived with one of my other families, I used to go out on the back porch at night and piss all over her roses. She never could figure out why they didn't do too good."

Seth was startled. It was the first time Daniel had ever mentioned anything about his past.

While Seth fixed the fire for the night, Daniel unrolled the sleeping bags. The boys undressed and climbed in. Each boy rolled his pants and shirt into a pillow. They settled down on the deep, soft bed of hemlock boughs, put their hands behind their heads, and lay staring at the fire.

A hermit thrush, startled awake, sang a short, interrupted song in the night and then was silent again. The boys joined the bird in sleep.

Morning came loud and early. At dawn, exactly dawn, long before the sun rose over the eastern mountains, the woods came alive with birds singing and chipmunks and squirrels scurrying about screeching argumentatively. The ravens, those rulers of sunrise, croaked over the treetops, flying back and forth above the mountains in a morning ritual the purpose of which was known only to themselves. Seth and Daniel climbed sleepy-eyed out of their bags and sat for a time in front of the lean-to shivering, waiting to wake up enough to start a fire.

Both boys felt happy. It looked as though it would be a good day.

After the fire was going well and they were waiting for it to settle to coals steady enough for cooking, Daniel began mixing pancake batter while Seth blended powdered milk, sugar, and cocoa for the morning's hot chocolate.

When breakfast was done and the pots and pans were washed and hung inside the lean-to, the boys constructed the fire pit and cooking range. They dug a shallow rectangular hole about two feet wide, four feet long, and four inches deep, in front of the reflector logs. They lined the hole with flat stones taken from the brook. The stones held heat and improved the range as a cooking surface. Two forked sticks about three feet high were stuck in the ground at either end of the range and a straight striped maple pole was cut and laid into the fork of each stick so that it stretched above the fire. Pots could be hung from the pole. With the cooking range complete the boys would be able to cook three or four separate dishes at once. They could complicate the menu now, begin to eat in style. Tonight they planned to have a real wilderness feast.

A few feet downstream from the camp Daniel found a small waterfall about three feet high and behind the falls, hollowed out of the ledge rock, a tiny cave about the size of a breadbox. It was exactly what he had been looking for: a refrigerator. Inside the tiny cave it was cold and damp, the perfect place to store their eggs, bacon, and extra trout. A little rearranging of stones and everything would be just right.

While Daniel worked on the ice box, Seth cut a straight branch from a young white ash tree and fashioned some fire utensils: a poker and a pair of tongs.

The poker was a simple matter; the tongs, however, required a lot of tooling and great care.

Seth began with a piece of ash about three feet long and two inches in diameter. First he flattened each end on what would be the inside. Then he whittled grooves in the flattened surface with his pocketknife to improve the grip. In the middle of the stick for about six inches either way from the center, he whittled down the diameter to about one third its original thickness. With this done, he built a small fire and began heating the thinned middle over the flames. As the green wood began to hiss and drip, he slowly and very carefully applied pressure to each end of the stick. Gradually the heat softened the cells in the wood and the stick began to bend under the pressure Seth applied until Seth was able to bend the tongs in so that each flattened, checked end touched the other. Tempered as it had been in the flames, the center did not break. Seth held the now completed pair of tongs above the fire for a moment, then dashed to the brook and plunged the hot tool into the icy water. He held it there until it was stone cold, then walked back to camp continuing to hold the two ends together. When the tongs were dry, he released the ends and they leaped open with the same definite liveliness as a fine piece of springy steel.

It was a lot of work, but Seth knew that a good pair of tongs was the most useful piece of fireplace hardware imaginable. With them he could lift hot pots, retrieve dropped pieces of food from glowing coals, rearrange burning firewood, and place hot coals exactly in the right position under a frying pan for even cooking. In a skillful hand tongs had the delicate accuracy of a pair of tweezers.

Daniel called Seth to see his craftily devised icebox, and after the proper compliments to Daniel's ingenuity, Daniel was obliged to walk back to camp to comment on the skill and craftsmanship with which Seth had fashioned their cooking tools.

These little touches, the icebox, the poker and tongs, were what made camp life enjoyable, made it something more than mere survival in the woods. The camp was their home, even if only for a short time, and like anyone proud of his home, the boys did everything they could to make it a good, pleasant, and livable place.

With the camp complete, the boys, swollen with the pride everyone feels for a thing well made, stood around and admired their handiwork. They puttered about the camp, pleased to be where they were.

Seth gathered and cut firewood while Daniel dug a toilet about fifty feet behind the camp. He dug a hole between two trees standing close together, deep enough to cover their waste well when they broke camp. With the hole dug, Daniel cut a smooth, round pole. He lashed it to each tree so that it passed over the hole about a foot and a half above the ground, making an improvised seat.

There was nothing else to do, so the boys made peanut butter sandwiches, gathered up the tea pail, a little sugar and tea, and their fishing tackle and headed upstream to the beaver pond they'd found the day before. They hopped from rock to rock, picking their way upstream. They felt good. Now the only vision that danced in either boy's head was one of huge trout.

The boys had a sorry disappointment waiting for them at the pond. They fished the deep areas all along the dam. They used worms, small lead-headed jigs, streamer flies, wet flies, dry flies, nymphs, but nothing worked. There wasn't even one little nibble.

"Guess we better head back downstream," Seth said.

"Yeah, I guess so," Daniel agreed. "Damn! We have the worst luck. Hey, wait a minute! I think I know what's wrong. This must be a dead pond. Look at that beaver house out there. It's covered with grass. There haven't been beavers in here for years. This

49[

water is too brackish, not enough oxygen. That's why
the water is so dark coming out of here, why there's
all that black moss below the dam. Trout won't live in
here."

"Maybe so," Seth said, "but we saw fresh beaver
cuttings down there."

"That's right, and that means there's beaver around
here somewhere. Hey! You know how beavers always
build dams in a series, one after another along a stream.
How much you want to bet there's another dam above
here. And a live pond, with trout in it. Those trout
in the brook have to come from somewhere."

"I'm not betting. Let's go!"

The boys gave the dormant pond a wide berth,
circled through a flat of hardwoods, found the inlet to
the pond, and poked their way upstream. Now there
were more and more fresh signs of beaver. Then,
ahead of them, there it was, a beaver pond four or
five times bigger than the one below. As the boys
climbed up over the dam, a startled muskrat plowed
his way through the skin of water.

"Look at that!" Daniel exclaimed. "Muskrat. A
fresh beaver house. This has got to be the place!"

It was. It didn't matter what the boys put on the
end of their lines; everything caught fish, and good-
sized ones too, some of them a foot long. Any deer

nearby must have gotten an odd eyeful that morning. There were two strange two-footed beasts pacing back and forth across the beaver dam, hooping and hollering, catching trout as fast as they could get their lines into the water. It was the kind of morning all fishermen dream of, but very few ever experience. Every cast, every single one, hooked a trout. No one must have ever fished the pond before. It was a trout fisherman's heaven. When the boys got home, no one would believe them, and they didn't care.

By lunch time each boy had caught dozens of trout, but they kept only two large ones apiece, just enough for lunch; all the rest they unhooked very carefully and returned gently to the water. They could get the trout they needed for supper during the afternoon fishing.

They found a good place for lunch near the edge of the pond and began gathering firewood. Suddenly Daniel called Seth over to a soft, muddy spot near the shore. There, printed neatly in the wet earth, was a bear track. The boys could tell by the sharp, clean lines of the track that it was fresh, probably last night's or even this morning's. The boys were more excited than frightened; in fact, neither had any fear of bears. There was little to be afraid of. If it were a she-bear with cubs and the boys got themselves between the mother and her babies, there could be trouble, but both Seth and Daniel knew that was highly unlikely. Bears were very shy and always gave humans plenty of room. Both boys actually hoped they would see the bear; they had lived around bears all their lives but had never seen one. However, they did decide then and there that when they returned to camp they would put all their food in one of the backpacks and hoist it by a length of baler twine high into a tree above the camp. A bear could wipe out their food supply and destroy the camp in a matter of minutes.

With the fire going, Seth stuck a stick into the damp earth so that it angled over the fire and then hung the tea pail full of water from the end of the stick. As the water heated, the boys ate their peanut butter sandwiches. When it boiled, Daniel dumped in the tea and set the pail aside while Seth began to roast the four trout he had skewered with a peeled green alder branch. The trout cooked quickly and soon were done. When lunch was finished, each boy propped himself up against a tree and stared quietly out across the beaver pond.

No beavers appeared that afternoon, but now and then a muskrat swam across the pond, busily doing something. A bright blue-and-white kingfisher swooped into the top of a drowned and naked spruce tree standing in the middle of the pond. The boys could see him cock his jauntily crested head to the side so that he could search the water below. Then, without warning, he dropped like a stone into the pond and disappeared completely under the water's surface. Soon he appeared again, and rose in a shower of silver drops above the pond and was gone over the tree tops, a large trout squirming helplessly in his beak.

"Roasting trout on a stick like that reminds me of the first time I ever did it," Daniel said dreamily. "It was five years ago. Dad and I were fishing the brook just above the swamp. It might have been the first thing we ever did together. Anyway, we caught a few and then we came on this little gravel bar in the brook. I was carrying the trout on a stick; we didn't have a creel that day. I remember it just like it was yesterday. I held the trout up and said, 'Boy, these look so good I'd like to eat them right now!' Dad just looked at me and said, 'Okay, wait a minute.' Before I knew what was going on, he had started a fire, and we were eating trout and drinking brook water. I don't know why that sticks in my head so clearly, but I bet when I'm as old as Mr. Bateau I'll still remember it like I do right now. And that place, that pool where we cooked the trout, I've never been there since, but

I can see it. I know *exactly* what it looks like. Man, that was some fun that day."

Both boys fell silent; they were tired. The lean-to camp was a comfortable place to spend the night, but no wilderness camp, not even a cozy one, offers as good a night's sleep as a soft bed in a warm house. A short nap was in order.

4

The afternoon's fishing began badly, and for a time the boys feared they wouldn't get enough fish for supper, but slowly their creels filled.

Seth pulled a writhing foot-long trout out of the pond, seized it, and cracked it once across the skull just above the eyes with a small, heavy stick, about six inches long, that he carried for killing fish. Both boys always killed the fish they meant to keep as soon as they caught them. It was cruel to drop live fish into a creel, where they would suffer an agonizing, slow death by suffocation. Death was involved in fishing just as it was in hunting, and the quicker and more efficient the killing could be the more acceptable that unsavory part of the game became. Seth watched the beautiful, lithe, red and black and yellow and purple and orange-speckled fish shiver its sudden way to death. Then it was still, cold on his palm. A small drop of blood appeared at the edge of the fish's mouth. Seth stared at the dead trout, and as he stared, he was carried back to a warm October afternoon last fall.

It was the first time his parents had allowed him to hunt partridge alone. Seth had hunted with his father many times, but as yet he had never actually killed a bird. Now he was on his own and he wanted more than anything to return home with a grouse or two to prove his skill as a hunter.

Seth poked his way along a hardwood ridge watching the trees for feeding birds who might sit tight, as they often did, and let him pass under them, then fly away behind him. He stopped now and then, waited, watched, and listened. All his senses were alive, on edge, in a way they had never been before. He saw things, heard things he would have missed had he not been hunting. His whole body hunted. He was sharp now, acute, the way a wild animal is all the time.

He pushed forward slowly, cautiously. Then, a few yards in front of him, a partridge exploded in a thunder of wings and shot upward into the branches of the trees. The gun exploded too. Instinctively, Seth had snapped the shotgun to his shoulder, pointed, and fired in the smallest fraction of a second.

The bird fell like a wad of dough. Seth ran forward, excited, frightened, amazed. Now he could hear his father saying, "Kill it quick! Grab its head and wring its neck. Don't make it suffer. Do the job and do it fast!"

But this first time he had to see, to watch; he had to know what death was, what it looked like. The bird lay thrashing in the dried leaves. It beat its wings faster, harder than it ever had in life. It opened its mouth slowly as if to say something, but no sound came out. Then behind each eye blood appeared and ran slowly down across the soft feathers of its face. The thrashing subsided to a shiver, the shiver to a tremble. Then the bird was still.

Seth held the warm, limp body in his hand. He started home.

He had proved his skill as a hunter, and over the years of his life he would prove it again and again, but he was not proud, not the way he had imagined he would be. Neither was he ashamed. As he loped down the logging road heading home, suddenly he felt older. In one afternoon he had become a great deal less a boy.

"Seth! Seth!" Daniel shouted.

Seth stood staring at the trout, the partridge, in his hand.

"Seth!"

"Huh?"

"What's the matter?"

"Oh, nothing."

With more than enough trout for supper the boys headed back to camp. About halfway there Daniel saw a familiar-looking plant growing in the stream: watercress. It was odd to find watercress growing so far from any human habitation. It usually grew only where someone planted it. The seeds must have been carried to the mountains from a village or a nearby farm in the droppings of a bird. The boys did not question their good fortune, however; instead, they picked a hearty bunch. They could make themselves a delicious salad to go with the feast they were now heading home to prepare.

It was only the middle of the afternoon, but there

was a lot of cooking to be done and they had to get started. Once back in camp they agreed on the evening's menu—fried trout, baked beans with onions, wilted watercress salad, club bread, and tea—and got to work.

While Seth started a fire, Daniel put about a half pint of shell beans in the two-quart pail and headed for the brook, where he washed and drained them thoroughly a number of times. When they were well cleaned, he added about a quart of water to the pail and returned to the fire. He hung the pail of beans and water from the cooking range cross pole. Soon it began to simmer. Daniel watched it carefully so that the beans would cook steadily, but not so rapidly that they'd stick to the bottom of the pail. As the beans began to dance in the moving water, he peeled and chopped an onion and added it. Later, after the beans began to soften, he'd add some potatoes, along with a few chunks of salt pork. It would take a couple of hours for the beans and potatoes to cook.

Meanwhile Seth had mixed flour, salt, sugar, and water in a pan and was kneading the concoction into a stiff dough. When the dough could be molded into a firm, springy ball, Seth set it aside and went into the woods. He cut and peeled a thick ash branch about four feet long, brought it back to camp, sharpened one end, and stuck it in the ground in front of the fire so that it angled above the coals. Then he molded the dough into a long ribbon about two inches wide and one-half inch thick. When the branch was sizzling hot, he wrapped the dough on a diagonal around and around it. As the dough began to brown over the coals, Seth turned the branch occasionally so that the bread baked evenly all around.

With the two long-cooking dishes for the meal started, the boys could relax and putter. Seth fussed with the fire, moving coals here and there with the tongs, adding a little wood now and then, while Daniel got out the improvised broom, a hemlock branch, and swept the "floor" in front of the camp. Both boys enjoyed hiking and fishing in new territory, but equally enjoyable was this time of hanging around camp, tending the pots, lazing about. There was a dazed, dreamy quality to times like these. The boys didn't talk much that afternoon; they found themselves slowly mesmerized by the smell of baking bread and beans wafting through the air around them. It was a time to think and dream, to listen to the sounds of the wilderness so different from the sound of their own voices.

When the potatoes and beans and club bread were

done, they were set off to the side of the fire, where they would stay warm but not cook. The boys snacked on the warm bread.

"Butter! Butter! My kingdom for some butter!" Daniel exclaimed.

While Seth put the trout to frying, Daniel melted a little bacon grease and poured it over the watercress to wilt and sweeten the sharp, tangy green. They ate, and what a feast it was! Both boys stuffed themselves; even with that there were plenty of leftovers that would be delicious cold the next day.

After they cleaned the dishes and pots, the boys set a pail of tea to boiling and hung the leftovers and the rest of their food in a tree. Even if a bear did smell the food and come by, it would be out of reach, and soon he would go off in a huff.

While the tea steeped the boys got out their map and planned the next day's hike to Eagle Ledge and Black Spruce. If they took a compass bearing of south 90 degrees west from the camp, they would arrive at the top of Eagle Ledge by the shortest route. If they struck off south 5 degrees east from there, they would drop down into the hollow between Eagle Ledge and Black Spruce and end up at the high, back side of the mountain. From there they could descend the western face to look for the cave they had heard about for years. By sticking to the compass bearing, they could walk in a straight line and reduce their travel time. According to the map it was only about a mile from their camp to the top of Eagle Ledge, but it would be hard climbing and would probably take most of the morning.

Both boys now felt the excitement of the adventure before them. The round trip would no doubt take the whole day, and they looked forward to doing something other than fishing.

There was nothing left of the day now. It was time to watch the final darkness fall down around them, while they sipped their tea, smoked their pipes, and let themselves be hypnotized by the evening fire. Then, out of the brook ravine below them came the clear call of a barred owl.

"Watch this," Daniel said.

He turned in the direction of the calling owl, cupped his hands around his mouth, and began making short, high, round noises from deep in his throat, little two-note jumps, four or five of them, followed by a descending, gravelly long note at the end. Daniel waited a long time, then repeated the call. The owl called again and so did Daniel. Another silence. Then the sound of the owl came from somewhere closer. Slowly, little by little, the owl moved up the ravine until, after what seemed like an eternity, the boys saw a dark form glide silently into a tree above the fire. There was no sound, not even the slightest rustle of wings. Seth's mouth dropped open.

"How did you do . . . "

At the sound of a human voice the owl dropped from its branch and disappeared into the dark trees.

"Seth!"

"Sorry."

"I'll never get him back now."

"How did you learn to do that?"

"I don't know. Just practice, I guess. I've been trying to call owls all summer. I worked on it a long time, until I got the sound just right. Then they started coming."

"That's amazing. Do you think he really thought you were another owl?" Seth asked.

"Nah. I think he was down in the ravine and he said to himself, 'There's some crazy kid up there trying to pretend he's an owl. I guess I'll go see what he looks like.' "

They heard the owl call from upstream near the beaver ponds. Daniel called back, but the owl would not answer.

"Let's go to bed," Seth suggested. "We've got a hard climb tomorrow, and who knows, maybe we'll find a cave with a skeleton in it. I bet we'll find old tools and bottles and all kinds of stuff too. Man, I can't wait. It's going to be so cool."

"Yeah" was all Daniel said.

The boys fixed the fire and climbed inside the lean-to. As they lay quietly, they heard the sound of coyotes in the night. First the full, round yap, then the long, descending wail of an adult animal, then the sudden frantic yips of puppies, four, maybe six little wild voices each at a different pitch eagerly trying to imitate their parents but not quite succeeding. The yipping grew and grew until the whole night filled with the raucous noise.

The boys smiled to themselves. They could see the two adults trying to go about the business of teaching their young to hunt while the puppies paid absolutely no attention but instead chased each other through the woods, tussling and wrestling in a comic mock battle far more interesting to them than the boring task of stalking a mouse.

The boys listened as the sound moved up Tamarack Brook and headed for the high ground around Morey's sugarhouse. It was beautiful night music.

Then suddenly from behind the lean-to, off toward Eagle Ledge, came a heart-stopping scream—not a howl, not a wail, but a scream, unlike any sound either boy had ever heard before. It was a horrifying, insane sound that gripped the boys with fear.

"What was that!" Seth whispered.

"I don't know."

Both boys lay frozen in their sleeping bags, too afraid to blink.

5

They didn't hear the scream again, but in the morning the sound still echoed through their minds.

"What do you think that was?" Seth asked.

"I don't know. I can't figure it out. I've heard bob-cats before and that wasn't any bobcat. I just don't know."

The boys let it go at that, but as they prepared and ate breakfast, the memory of the scream hung over them like a bad dream bringing with it a vague but persistent fear of the day to come.

In spite of their apprehensions they finished breakfast and packed one backpack for the trip. Lunch would be leftovers from last night's supper. Along with the food they put into the pack the fifty-foot length of rope, the flashlight, and two candles, just in case they might be needed. Neither boy was really convinced they'd find a cave, but if they did, they'd need some light.

After the camp had been tidied and the fire well doused, the boys struck off on their predetermined compass bearing. It wasn't long before they began the difficult ascent up the northern side of Eagle Ledge.

The slope was so steep that the boys had to zigzag across the hillside, moving from tree to tree. Some places where it was particularly steep, they had to seize tree trunks and bushes and move hand over hand in order to make any upward progress. It was a dangerous game. Each small tree had to be inspected before they took hold of it; a dead, rotten tree could give way under the strain and send the boys tumbling down the hillside. On a slope this steep even a short fall might mean serious injury. When they finally reached a plateau near the top, both boys collapsed exhausted onto a soft bed of pine needles beneath the windswept trees.

They could see now that from where they were it

was less than a hundred yards up a gentle slope to the top. They pushed on. They were sure that when they gained the summit they would be able to see a hundred miles in any direction. But when they got there, they found that the top of Eagle Ledge was still well below the tree line and the thick-set spruce and fir blocked their view. They were disappointed. Seth climbed a small spruce.

"Don't give up yet, Daniel. I can see the top of Black Spruce from here. When we get up there, we'll be able to see the whole world. Let's get going."

Now they had to descend into the high, shallow basin that lay between Eagle Ledge and Black Spruce Mountain. When they reached the bottom of the basin, they found a small rivulet.

"I'm getting hungry," Daniel said. "Let's follow this stream up a little ways. Maybe we can find the spring that starts it and have lunch there. It must be almost noon."

A few hundred feet farther up the tiny brook, the rivulet disappeared completely. Daniel began shuffling around in the leaves with his feet looking for the wet place that meant the spring. Suddenly one leg dropped a full two feet, well above his knee, into a deep hole filled with water.

"Ugh, I found the spring!" Daniel said.

"Guess you did," Seth said, laughing, as Daniel pulled his dripping leg out of the water. "Let's clean it out and have lunch. By the time we finish eating, the water will be clear enough to make tea."

"Something's funny here," Daniel said.

"What do you mean?"

"In a place like this a spring always makes a big soggy area where it comes out of the ground, not just one deep hole."

The boys began cleaning the spring, raking away leaves with their hands and scooping out twigs and muck.

"Hey, wait a minute!" Seth exclaimed. "Feel the sides. This spring's been dug out and stoned up!"

The boys felt, through the water, the carefully placed, circular stone wall of a small well.

"Who would go to all the trouble of digging out this spring and stoning up a well?" Seth asked.

"Maybe some hunter."

"That's an awful lot of work just to get a drink."

"Maybe there were some campers here once. That's possible," Daniel said.

"I guess."

The boys unpacked lunch and ate. By the time lunch was over, the water in the small well had cleared and the boys dipped a pail into the well and made tea.

It had been a hard morning's climb, and they needed a cup of tea and a short rest before beginning their assault on the mountain.

Near the well, stuck like a wart on the side of the basin wall, was a small bulge in the earth about eight feet broad and eight feet high. Daniel settled himself against it while Seth puttered with the last of the fire. As Daniel scrunched around to get comfortable, he suddenly fell backward into a room, a cave inside the bulge. He rolled over quickly and backed out.

"Seth! Get the flashlight!"

"What?"

"Get the flashlight!"

Hurriedly the boys cleared away the debris from the opening and crawled in. They turned on the light. They were in a small room, maybe six feet wide by six feet long by four feet high. They could see the old logs that had been laid against the basin wall to make the room. This thing was no accident. It was man-made. Or maybe boy-made.

The flashlight scanned the ceiling, the walls, then the floor. There in the corner was an old shovel and next to it, covered with dust, an old glass canning jar.

"Daniel, how did . . . "

Both boys were stunned. They crouched in the center of the dark barrow while the realization of where they were swept through them like a chilling wind.

The first year, in the fall, some canning jars of vegetables and meat disappeared from the cellar and a couple of horse blankets and an old pair of woolen pants disappeared from the barn. . . . Then the second year no food or clothing disappeared, but a shovel and a hoe came up missing.

"I'll get the candles," Seth said.

With the candles lighted and set around the barrow in the loose dirt of the floor, the boys, without saying a word, began searching every inch of the now well-lighted room. The remains of an old horse blanket, the blade of a hoe, a few more canning jars, a small can of nails.

The story was true!

Although they had found almost all the things they'd ever heard about in the story, the boys kept searching, looking for that final, absolute confirmation that it was true. Carefully their fingers raked through the dust of generations. Here and there they came upon another piece of metal or a small fragment of cloth, but no skeleton.

When every inch of the room had been combed, the boys crawled out of the barrow and sat shaken, their eyes squinting in the brilliant light of day.

"I can't believe it. I just can't believe it," Seth said. "It's true! The story's true!"

"Well, not all of it."

"What do you mean?"

"We didn't find the bones, did we?"

"No, we didn't, but we know he was here. We know he spent a few years here."

"We do not! We've got no proof he spent a winter here. He just couldn't."

"Maybe he slept. I mean hibernated, like a bear."

"All winter? Come on, Seth!"

"Why not?"

"Because a bear's got a bearskin coat to sleep in. That kid didn't."

"How do you know? Maybe he killed a bear and made himself a bearskin to sleep in."

"Holy cow, Seth, you should write adventure stories. You've got the imagination for it."

"Really. Maybe he did make it. I've read about how some people can slow their bodies down like they're dead, like a woodchuck. Maybe he did that."

"Come on."

"Well, we've got proof he lasted more than one winter. We found stuff Mr. Bateau said was stolen the second and third year. That proves he survived up here."

"It does not!" Daniel said. "Maybe Mr. Bateau got things mixed up. It was a long time ago and people forget the truth. Maybe the kid stole all that stuff the first fall. The kid could have taken all that stuff, gotten ready for winter, and then when he realized he couldn't make it, he took off, went away somewhere, took up with some people."

"That's crazy."

"Why? It could have happened that way. Maybe the kid got out. Maybe he found a family, somebody to take him in."

"Daniel, you're just making up a story! You're ignoring all the facts."

"I am not! If you're so interested in the facts, tell me where the bones are. Where did they go?"

"Maybe an animal dragged them off, maybe somebody stole them. I don't know what happened to them, and you don't either. I just think he survived up here."

"What've you got against the kid escaping?" Daniel demanded. "He's got as much right as anybody to have a family, doesn't he? What've you got against him finding somebody to live with?"

"I've got nothing against it! You just keep refusing to believe the story. You've been fighting the truth since the first day. It's all true and you know it; you're just too pigheaded to admit it! What's it take to make you believe?"

"A lot more! A damn lot more!"

There was a long silence. Then Daniel began again.

"Seth, look, pretend just for a minute, pretend he got all ready to spend the winter up here and then he took off, to Canada, say, where he could start life over again. He found a family . . . "

"You already said that."

"I know, I know. But just pretend that's what happened. They took him in and he grew up like any other kid."

"But how could he just *find* a family?"

"I don't know! He just could, that's all!"

"Okay," Seth said, "I'll admit it looks like the kid did get away, but that stuff about his finding a family is ridiculous. Why do you like it? It's crazy."

"Not to me. It's not crazy to me. I can't explain it. I just like thinking about it that way."

"Well, I still don't get it."

Daniel put on the backpack. "There's no point in talking about this anymore. Come on, let's go."

6

Seth leveled the compass in the palm of his hand and waited for the needle to stop rotating. "What's that bearing we're supposed to take?" he asked.

"South 5 degrees east."

"Yeah. Looks good. It should take us up over the side of the basin. If we go due west when we get up there, we ought to hit the summit pretty close."

They moved up out of the basin and headed toward the back side of the mountain. The fear and apprehension the boys had felt earlier that day were gone.

The discovery of the barrow, the old tools and jars, the pieces of blanket, had answered the nagging, anxious questions that had hovered in the backs of their minds. But what made them feel good, especially Daniel, was their failure to find the bones. It took the terror out of the story, bled it of its horror. The boys could relax and enjoy the rest of the hike. It was a beautiful day, and as they headed for the top of the mountain, they were in high spirits.

"You know, Seth, that place must be the one Mr. Bateau's father found. Probably there's not even a cave up on the mountain. Nobody could live up there anyway; it's too exposed to the weather. The story must have gotten all mixed up over the years."

"I think you're right, Daniel. Yes, I think that's right. Maybe we should go back and go fishing or something."

"Nah. We're up this far, let's keep going. I've always wanted to see the view from up there anyway."

Ever since the boys had reached the top of Eagle Ledge, ravens had been fussing in the air above them, croaking worriedly over the two intruders into their domain. It was raven country, high and far away, and the big black birds were not used to humans. All morning the boys had been too nervous about what they might find to notice the birds, but now, with their questions answered, they watched the birds circle above them, listened to the enormous variety of croaks and caws of raven talk.

"Hey, look at this!" Seth reached down and plucked an enormous black feather off the ground, a primary raven feather from a wing, almost twelve inches long, the biggest feather either boy had ever seen.

"Neat!" Daniel exclaimed.

The boys heard a pair of ravens talking to one another nearby. "Here's another trick for you," Daniel said, and as he had done with the owl, he cupped his hands around his mouth and began talking back. First some deep raspy caws that sounded like a crow with laryngitis. Then a *blonk, blonkblonk, blonkblonk* that sounded for all the world like someone hammering on a metal pipe. Then the caws again.

Suddenly two enormous ravens appeared overhead and, seeing the boys, frantically beat their wings to brake themselves; then, in a hiss, a rush of wings, they wheeled and soared away.

The boys could hear the ravens chattering to each other as they flapped out of sight, discussing what they must have thought was their narrow escape.

"Did you see that, Daniel! One of them had a feather missing from a wing." Seth stood staring at the feather in his hand, his eyes wide with wonder.

Seth and Daniel moved up the gently sloping back of the mountain toward the summit. The higher they got, the more stunted the trees became and the less ground cover there was. Now they were surrounded by spruce and fir less than ten feet high, but ancient nonetheless. In this windswept, rocky place growth was slow.

Then there were no trees at all and the soil gradually thinned out until the boys walked on rock covered only by prehistoric green and gray lichen that clung tenaciously to the enormous outcroppings of granite ledge. Slowly, gingerly, the boys clambered over one enormous rock after another. At last they found themselves standing on a huge, flat-topped boulder, balanced there by a glacier ten thousand years before. There was nowhere else to go; the whole world lay beneath them.

They looked down a hundred feet to the tops of trees. They saw a hawk soaring below them and for the first time in their lives they could see its back, the top of its wings. They watched the hawk tilt this way and that as it searched the ground far below.

Both boys suddenly experienced a wild and giddy desire to dive off the rock, spread their arms, and soar like the hawk below. It was a compelling urge, and both felt a kind of lightheadedness they'd never known before. They stepped back a little.

They turned to the south and looked down the side of the mountain to the valley below. They saw the village of Hardwick, the place the boy had run away from, tucked in its valley like a toy town surrounded by trees that, from where the boys were, looked like soft green smoke.

They looked east up the jagged spine of mountains toward Canada and the larger, more ominous mountains that dwarfed the rock they stood on.

North, out across Lost Boy Brook ravine, was Seth's farm, a small, smooth place with house and barn, carved out of the jungle of trees.

They looked west down over the treacherous crag, the western face of the mountain, to the fields and meadows surrounding Daniel's farm. They could see Mr. Bateau's house farther down the road. And deep in the heart of Bear Swamp they saw the beaver pond where they had fished last summer glittering in the sun.

Then their eyes rose and soared over hills and plains, sixty miles west to the blurred, crooked ribbon of Lake Champlain.

Seth and Daniel stood awestruck. The world looked so big! Everything human looked so small. They had always thought of their farms as tiny, open places in a vast sea of trees. But what they now understood was how small they themselves were, how insignificant and meaningless their tiny bodies seemed in this endless landscape. They were ants, mere mites, scuttling across the face of the earth.

After a long time they eased themselves down off the boulder and inched toward the edge of the cliff.

"Well, are we going over the side?" Daniel asked.

"Jeez, I don't know," Seth answered. "It's scarier up here than I thought."

"I know, but since we're up here, we might as well give it a try."

The top of the mountain was not as steep as it seemed from lower down. As the boys peeked over the edge, they could see a ledge six or eight feet wide about twenty feet below them. Below the ledge, however, the rock face dropped sheer and straight for a hundred feet. The trip from the ledge on down was only for a bird.

"What do you think?" Daniel asked.

"Let's do it. But let's use the rope. We can hitch it up here someplace and throw it over the side. I don't think we'll need it, but if we do, it'll be there."

The boys tied a jagged rock to one end of the rope, and wedged the rock and rope into a small crevice in the mountain. They tested it to make sure it was secure, then tossed the coil into the air and watched it open, writhing like a snake as it fell to the ledge below.

Now, as the boys stood trying to screw up their courage, they noticed far to the west, over the big lake, banks of black thunder clouds building in the sky.

"Looks like rain," Seth said.

"Yeah, but it's a long way off. Probably a couple of hours. Let's get going. We can get down and back before it hits."

The boys inched their way down the rock face, never getting more than an arm's length away from each other. It was tricky but not really very danger-ous. There were lots of footholds and handholds all the way down, and although the going was slow, they felt secure—until Seth happened to turn away from the rock and look out across the plateau far below. Suddenly the giddy urge to fly that Seth had felt at the top turned to a paralytic fear.

"Daniel, I can't move!"

"What?"

"I can't move."

"What do you mean?"

"I mean I just can't! I looked down. I'm scared."

"Okay. Take it easy. We'll go back up."

"I can't. I can't go up or down."

"Let's rest a minute. Look straight at the rock. Don't look around. Take it easy."

Daniel talked to Seth in reassuring tones and slowly Seth felt the stiffness ease out of his body. He began to relax.

They were stuck there a long time however, and the dark clouds had moved steadily eastward. The wind began to blow a little.

They began their descent again, and finally, after what seemed like hours but was in fact only a matter of minutes, they found themselves standing on the flat ledge twenty feet below the summit.

The ledge was broader than it had appeared from above, and as the boys moved easily along it, they came to a place where it deepened under an enormous rock overhang. Here the flat ledge was a good twelve or fifteen feet wide. The rock overhang jutted out and away above it, making a roof over the ledge. It was a perfect place to camp.

From here the view was blocked in every direction but west. The boys could still see the big lake far in the distance, but what fascinated them now was the view of Daniel's farm. It seemed closer, more intimate, as if the boys were hovering in the sky directly over it.

"Daniel, there's your dad!"

"Where?"

"He's plowing in the meadow behind the barn. See him?"

"I'll be darned. He said he was going to start that sometime this week. We're going to put it to corn in the spring."

Daniel could see his father on the tractor, moving across the meadow, the whole scene in miniature beneath him.

"Hello!" Seth shouted.

"He'll never hear you. That old John Deere makes so much noise, he wouldn't hear you if you were shouting in his ear."

The boys sat for a long time watching. They could see a dark line, the damp, rich earth of the turned furrow, follow the tractor back and forth across the field.

The rain clouds continued to build. They were moving eastward even more rapidly than before. The wind blew a little harder. Then somewhere to the west there was a vague rumble of thunder.

Daniel gave up watching his father, left Seth at the edge, and began poking along the back of the ledge. A little farther down the flat place there was a rubble of rocks broken and fallen away from the overhang by centuries of freezing and thawing. There was a small open place in the pile of rocks. Daniel reached through. His hand grabbed air. He began clearing away the stones until he had an opening large enough to slip through. Daniel crawled in.

"Daniel?"

"I'm in here."

"Where?"

"Over here. There's a cave back in here."

"Can you see?"

"Some."

"Want the flashlight?"

"Nah."

Daniel crawled farther into the darkness of the cave; his hands and knees shuffled through the dust. Then his hand came to rest on something smooth and round. It felt like a stone, but not exactly like a stone. He ran his fingers over it. At the top there was a smooth, broad area, then two round holes side by side below the smooth place, then another triangular hole centered below them, then two rows of something that felt . . . like teeth.

Daniel couldn't breathe.

Then, calmly, Daniel said, "Seth, bring the flashlight."

7

Seth scurried on all fours into the dark cave. He flipped on the flashlight. "Oh, God!"

There it was, half buried in dust, the skeleton of a boy.

"Daniel, let's get out of here! Oh, shit, let's get out of here!"

Seth dropped the flashlight and headed for the opening. Daniel, however, sat still, hunkered down in the dust and dark of the cave. He didn't move; he didn't speak; he sat there and stared at the boy's bones.

"Daniel, come on!"

But Daniel didn't hear Seth; he didn't hear anything. He was lost, somewhere inside himself.

"*Daniel!*"

As Seth climbed onto the open ledge, an enormous bolt of lightning struck the mountaintop. The whole mountain shook. The sky was thick and black. Thunder rolled back and forth through the clouds. The trees below tossed in the wind.

"Daniel! Come on! There's a storm coming. Come on!"

Daniel didn't answer.

Then the rain hit. Great sheets of rain and hail lashed the mountainside. The terrible wind and rain drove Seth back toward the opening to the cave. There, under the overhang, he was protected. He stood trembling, looking out through a wall of water pouring down off the mountain above. There was no chance now of getting back up the mountain. If they tried, the wind would pick them up like leaves and blow them away. They were trapped.

In a daze Daniel emerged from the cave, propped himself up against the opening, and stared out into the storm without saying anything, oblivious to everything around him.

"What's the matter with you, Daniel? Have you gone crazy?"

"Nope," Daniel said softly.

"What's the matter?"

"I'll tell you later." Daniel was still somewhere else. After a long time Daniel reached back into the cave and pulled an object out into the light. "Look at this."

He held a crude spear in his hands made from a stick and the knife off a cutter bar.

"It was his weapon, his protection. Look, Seth, look at it. This wasn't for hunting bear. This was to keep him safe from the others."

"What are you talking about!"

Then, as if he had just finished a big meal and was about to get up from the table, Daniel said, "Well, now what?"

"Now what! Now we're getting out of here!"

"You know we're not. We're stuck. We're not going anywhere."

"We've got to get out of here! I'm going even if you aren't!"

"Seth, get hold of yourself. It's suicide to climb back up now and you know it. I don't want to die and I don't think you do either. Sit down. We're going to wait for a break in the storm. It can't rain this hard for long. Sit down. It's just some bones. They're not going to throw a spear at you. That kid got rid of his troubles a long time ago."

Daniel's calm began to have its effect. Slowly Seth began to see the situation with clearer eyes. They would have to wait, and that was that.

"This spear is amazing," Daniel said. "See how he split the end of the shaft and bound the knife in with wire? He could have killed a bear or a deer, but I bet he didn't.

"He took it wherever he went. It was always with him. It guarded him. Like our belt knives; we don't really need them, but we feel safer when we've got them."

Daniel was so certain, so positive about his explanation, that Seth thought it must be true.

As so often happens with summer storms, the rain stopped and the clouds began to disperse. The boys knew enough not to hope the storm was over. It would begin again, but the lull gave Seth and Daniel a chance to try their escape.

The climb back up the cliff went quickly, and although the rocks were wet, neither boy slipped.

When the boys reached the top, they found the bare, stony summit covered with an inch of hailstones. They were melting rapidly, but the footing was hard and slippery. Seth and Daniel inched their way through the ice and soon were moving over soil and under trees. The sky was darkening again, getting ready to let down another torrent. And now, to add to their troubles, it was growing dark. In the excitement and terror of the afternoon the boys had not noticed the day slip away. It was well past suppertime, but eating was the farthest thing from their minds. All either boy could think about was getting back to camp. They wanted more than anything just now to be in the place that had become their home.

"Let's get out the map, Seth. We've got to find a short cut. It's almost dark."

According to the map if they could hold a bearing of east 10 degrees north they would be able to pass around the back side of Eagle Ledge and strike the first small beaver pond where they had been two days ago. It would be farther that way but much quicker, for there would be no climbing. The topographical rings on the map indicated fairly level going. They got their bearing and took off.

Because of the heavy clouds, dark came sooner than it would have under a clear sky. Soon it was too dark to read the compass.

"I can't see this thing anymore," Daniel said. "Get the flashlight."

Seth rummaged in the backpack. "It's not here."

"Oh, damn! I left it in the cave."

"What are we going to do? Why did you leave it!"

"Seth, I don't know. This is no time for an argument! We've got to get home. The only thing we can do is just feel our way along, I guess."

The instinct that had carried them correctly to Morey's sugarhouse that first day was useless now: it was dark, and they were in new country. Luck was all they had to go on.

The thunder began again, and the rain. Suddenly, not more than fifty feet in front of them a bolt of lightning struck a huge spruce tree and split it in half. A terrible clap of thunder followed immediately. The explosion was so deafening, the boys staggered backward at the noise. Again the intense white light flashed, and sparks danced the length of the tree; then the whole top of the tree burst into flame, tottered, and began to fall toward the boys.

They dove away from the falling fire. The tree shook the earth when it hit, sending a brilliant shower of orange sparks and fiery branches blowing through the woods.

When it was safe to look, the boys leapt up and began running through the woods. All reason was gone. Luck had deserted them and fear possessed them. They ran, panting, dripping wet; somewhere, anywhere. They were lost, and they ran.

"*Daniel!*"

Daniel wheeled. In another flash of light he saw Seth lying on his side, gripping his leg with both hands.

"I'm hurt. I fell. I cut my leg."

Seth had tripped—a sharp rock. Now a deep gash oozed blood along his shin. Daniel felt in the darkness through Seth's torn pants. His fingers met the warm, thick blood.

"I think it's bad," Daniel said.

Daniel opened his pocket knife and cut Seth's pants from above the knee down to the cuff. He wrapped his bandana around the wound and tied it tight.

"Can you stand?"

"I think so."

Seth stood up.

"It hurts."

"Okay. Put your arm around my shoulder. I'll be your bad leg. Let's go."

"Where? We don't know where we are."

"I know. Let's start moving anyway. Maybe we'll luck out."

The accident had brought both boys back to their senses. Now that they were in real danger, their heads settled. They set out calmly, determined to find their way, one limping and leaning on the other.

Another flash of lightning lit up the woods and Daniel saw straight in front of him a small beaver pond, *the* beaver pond.

"We're okay, Seth. I know where we are."

Seth's teeth were clenched together. "Good" was all he said.

The two boys staggered downstream toward their camp. Seth was growing heavier and heavier. Daniel's back ached. Finally they were home.

For a moment Daniel imagined that the lost boy was waiting for them at the camp, that he had a fire going, supper hot and waiting, their sleeping bags rolled out, everything warm and cozy. Then Daniel saw the scene the way it really was. The camp stood dark and soaking in the night. It looked good anyway.

The boys hobbled into the lean-to and collapsed on the soft bed of hemlock boughs. Daniel lighted two candles. The glow filled and warmed the tiny wilderness room. It was almost like being in a kitchen on a cold winter night, the wood stove going, the air full of the smell of doughnuts and coffee.

"Get your clothes off," Daniel said. "I'll get the first-aid kit."

Daniel gently cleaned and dressed the wound.

"It's not as bad as I thought. Pretty deep, but it bled a lot, probably won't be too sore."

"Thanks, Daniel," Seth said, and as he said it, his hand reached out to touch Daniel, but before it could reach him it hesitated and then returned to Seth's side.

"It's okay. Let's get some sleep."

Both boys zipped themselves into their bags and lay listening to the now gentle rain whispering on the lean-to roof.

Gradually Daniel became aware that Seth was crying, soft sobs welling up from somewhere deep inside him.

"What's the matter?"

"I want to go home!"

8

Sometime during the middle of the night, Daniel didn't know exactly when, he woke. The storm was gone and what clouds remained raced across the sky under a full moon.

Daniel was wide awake and very hungry. He got up, went out back to the toilet, then returned and started a fire. He felt around in the refrigerator down at the brook and found one piece of bacon and two trout. There was still a little club bread left. He cooked supper.

"Seth . . . Seth." Daniel shook him gently. "How's your leg?"

"Huh?" Seth raised himself on an elbow. "Okay. It doesn't hurt."

"Want supper?"

"Now? What time is it?"

"I don't know. Two, three o'clock."

"Why not? I'm starved."

"It's all ready."

Seth crawled out of the lean-to and stood up. "My leg feels pretty good. It's a little stiff. Probably I'll limp some, but it feels all right."

The boys ate in silence. Seth was sleepy; Daniel was thinking.

"We got any coffee?" Daniel asked. "I'm sick of tea."

Seth rummaged inside the lean-to. "We brought enough for one pot."

"Good. I'll mix some milk."

The panic of the day was gone. They sat staring at the fire, drinking hot coffee with milk. It was good to be back in camp, good to be safe.

"Well," Daniel said, "I admit it. The story *is* true, every bit of it, just the way they tell it. It didn't get mixed up at all."

"Yeah, it is. I was so anxious for it to be true; I

don't know why, but now that I know it *is* true, I'm not glad."

Seth was silent for a moment, then he continued:

"Only they didn't know the whole story. Nobody ever mentioned the mound or the well. I think we were the first ones to find that place. I don't think Mr. Bateau's father was ever there. He must have only found the cave on the mountain. Maybe you're right, Daniel; maybe he did die that first winter; maybe he stole all that stuff the first fall."

"I don't think so. I've changed my mind. I think he survived, for a couple of years at least."

"But we can't prove that."

"Maybe we can," Daniel argued. "There's got to be something in all that stuff we found that proves he lasted more than one year."

"That watercress we found," Seth said, "I bet he planted that, stole it and planted it."

"Maybe he did, but he could have done that the first fall."

"Yeah. The jars and clothes he could have gotten the first fall too, even though the story says different."

"That's right, but I just don't see how he could have done it all in one fall. He built that mound to live in, that was a big job, and he stoned up the well. He must have spent a lot of time going around stealing things. And if he learned to hunt with that spear, he must have spent weeks, maybe months, learning how to sneak up on game before he ever got anything. It all seems like too much to learn, too much to do, in a few months."

"I know it. I wonder where he learned it all."

"He taught himself," Daniel asserted. "He had to."

"I guess so. You know," Seth mused, "it's like he was building a whole new civilization up here."

"Only there was one thing missing."

"What?"

"Other people," Daniel said.

The boys fell silent, thinking, trying to find that one clue that would prove beyond doubt that the boy had lived in the mountains more than one fall.

Seth got up, poured himself some more coffee, and began limping back and forth in front of the fire. Suddenly he turned toward Daniel and exclaimed, "The hoe!"

"What?"

"The hoe! What's the only thing you use a hoe for?"

"Hoeing."

"Hoeing what?"

A smile flashed across Daniel's face. "A garden! And he was too late the first year to have a garden. He could only have had a garden after the first winter up here."

"Ah, it's no good," Seth said. "He could have taken the hoe the first fall figuring he'd have a garden. Then he could have died before he had the chance."

"Maybe so," Daniel said, "but I'm ready to believe. Maybe we won't ever be able to prove he really did survive, but I think he did, at least I want to think he did."

"How come you've changed your mind all of a sudden?"

"I don't know. It's just a feeling, ever since I saw the bones. I know that boy."

Daniel stood up and began pacing back and forth in front of the fire. His hands gestured nervously in front of him.

"He . . . he feels like my brother. When I close my eyes I can see him up here, moving around like a wild animal. I can imagine what he thought, how he felt."

"Okay, then," Seth asked, "if you know all about it, what killed him? If he didn't freeze or starve, what killed him?"

"Nothing. He wasn't killed; he died. And it's just like Mr. Bateau said, he died of loneliness."

"What?"

"Those bones were lying there just as if he'd died in his sleep. They weren't messed up or broken or anything: they were just lying there, all stretched out. One night he just gave up and died."

"I don't get it."

"Don't you see, Seth? The boy was an orphan."

Daniel's voice began to tremble. "He probably never even knew who his parents were. He knocked around from here to there; he never really had a home. Then he got hooked up with that guy in Hardwick who beat him all the time. You can only stand so much of that."

As Daniel talked, he could feel himself slipping farther and farther back into his own past.

"You can only live so long without anybody to love you, and then something snaps, you get a little crazy or something. You get so you can't trust anybody, even though you want to. After that happens, even though you want to trust people and you want people to trust you, even though you want that more than anything in the world, you can't. I think that's what happened to the boy. It got too late for him. That's why he ran away. And that's why he never came down off the mountain. He couldn't. He wanted to, but he couldn't. He was just too afraid of other people."

"You mean he went crazy, just like Mr. Bateau said."

Daniel sat down abruptly and sighed a frustrated sigh. He let his chin droop into his chest and he stared at the darkened ground between his feet.

"Sure he went crazy, if that's what you want to call it."

Then suddenly Daniel stood up and threw his arms out toward Seth.

"But he couldn't help it! Can't you see! He didn't want to be up here. But it was the only thing left. He *hated* living up here. He was lonely and afraid!"

Daniel started to pace back and forth in front of the fire again.

"Look, most kids would think it takes a lot for a boy to live alone like an animal on a mountain. It does. . . . It does, but it didn't take half as much courage as it would have for him to come down. You see? Coming down would have meant trusting someone. And he couldn't. He just couldn't do that. So he lived up here until he couldn't stand it anymore and then he just gave up and died. He was trapped. He was too afraid to come down and too lonely to live."

"I can't imagine being *that* lonely."

"I know you can't. I mean, it's hard for you to understand, maybe impossible. You've never known what it's like to be completely alone, even when there are other people around, not to have anybody to belong to, anybody you can trust. You've always had your parents, since the day you were born."

Daniel stopped for a moment, reached into the darkness outside the firelight and picked up a stick. He slapped his empty, open palm with the stick and looked away somewhere into his past. Then he laughed a tight, bitter little laugh and began to pace again.

"You don't know what it's like. Before I was eight years old I'd been in twelve different places. I remember the last place I stayed before I came here. I'd been there a long time, I don't know how long. It was awful. I got blamed for everything. So one day I took off, just like the boy, only I was a little kid, eight. It was winter, but I took off anyway. I had my sneakers on. I got maybe a mile or so down the road and there I was, nowhere. Where could I go? So I turned around and went back. They weren't even out looking for me. They were sorry to see me back."

"How do you know that?"

"*I just know it!*"

Daniel waited a minute to cool down. "They didn't give me hell or anything; they just looked at me, just stared at me. They didn't say anything. I remember that. None of them even blinked. They just stared. I knew then I wasn't long for *that* place and I was right. About a month later the social worker came and got me and brought me up here."

"You never told me any of that," Seth said.

"I've never told *anybody anything* about those days. I don't talk about them because I want to forget them. I want to forget the first eight years of my life. I want to forget the whole thing. But I can't! I try, but I can't forget."

Seth didn't know what to say, so he said, "Well, at least when you came here you knew you were coming to stay."

A sharp, angry laugh shot out of Daniel's mouth. "I knew you were dumb, Seth, but I didn't know you were *that* dumb."

Daniel's cruelty hurt Seth. He wanted to say something, but he couldn't speak.

"You're hopeless. You'll never know what I'm talking about. Coming here was *worse* than staying there. How was I to know they were going to keep me? How was I to know? All I knew was it was another place to stay for a while, get kicked around, get kicked out."

"You make it sound like your folks were going to treat you like a stray dog!"

"No kidding."

Seth was beginning to understand a little the depth, the fury, of Daniel's bitterness.

"But you knew they were going to adopt you! They said they were."

"Said? Said! Shit! Listen, you don't believe what people say. You don't believe *anything* they say. People talk all the time. What good are words? Words are just words!

"When I first came here everybody got all excited. Your folks, my folks, you, Mr. Bateau, everybody; everybody but *me*." Daniel jabbed his forefinger hard into his chest.

"I remember how your mother jumped around when she first met me. She acted like an idiot. I thought she was crazy. And your sister trying to hold me on her lap! A new toy. I felt like telling all of you to save it. When your father came up to me and put out his hand and said, 'Daniel, I'm glad to meet you,' when he said that, do you know what I wanted to do? I wanted to look right up into his face and say, '*You go to hell!*' All that talk didn't mean squat to me. I didn't believe it. Like a stray dog you said? That's *exactly* what I felt like."

Daniel's whole body was shaking. Then in a voice

so bitter and angry that it became soft, Daniel said, "Only stray dogs don't move around twelve times in eight years."

Seth stared at the ground between his legs, "God."

There was a deep silence between the two boys for a time; then, in a voice filled with pleading and tenderness, Seth said, "But . . . isn't it better now? I mean, you've been here five years. They really *are* your parents. They really *do* love you. Isn't it better now?"

It was a long time before Daniel answered. "Yes . . . it is . . . a little. It's a little better. But no matter how hard I try to forget, I can still *remember*. That's no better, and it never will be either."

It wasn't what Seth had hoped to hear.

"There's only one difference between me and that boy, Seth. Just one."

"What's that?"

"I lucked out. He didn't."

Both boys sat in silence for a time. Then Daniel began again. His voice had changed because his anger was gone, not gone away from him, but gone back down into him.

"That's why I didn't want to believe the story. It was just too terrible to be true. I *had* to refuse to believe it. I just couldn't admit it was true, not even the tiniest bit, because . . . ah! I don't know how to say it . . . because . . . the story could have been about me!

"Don't you see, Seth? If I hadn't lucked out, if I'd kept running, that boy could have been me!"

Then, abruptly, in a voice that made Seth shiver, Daniel said, "No more! I don't want to talk about this anymore!"

Daniel sat slumped and sullen. Seth tried to think of something to say, some question to ask, something, anything, to help Daniel escape from his memories.

"How come he had two places? How come we found all his stuff one place and his bones another?" Seth asked.

Daniel smiled. He knew what Seth was trying to do and he was grateful.

"I think the cave was his lookout. He could have found that place first and hid there while the search parties were looking for him. Then he built that mound, but he always went back to the cave because he could look down from there on the farm. He could see people. Maybe he even spent the whole summer there, sort of like a summer place. That explains the howls."

"How does it do that?"

"You know how people used to say they'd hear howls from the mountain only in the summer during haying? Well, probably the boy sat up there and watched. You know haying is the most sociable time of year, when everybody gets together. The boy watched all those people working together all day, sweating out in the sun and then when the hay was in, when they got together and had a big dinner on the lawn—he probably could hear them talking and laughing if the wind was right—when he saw all that and heard all that, he got so lonely he'd howl, because he felt so deserted. He wanted to come down and be a part of that, but he couldn't; so he howled instead."

Daniel could hear the boy's cries. He could see him alone on the mountain.

"I think he died during haying, just like Mr. Bateau says. I think one night, after he'd spent all day watching, he just couldn't stand it anymore, so he crawled into the cave and died."

"I think you're right, Daniel, but it's awful."

Both boys sat hunched over their thoughts.

Finally Daniel sighed an enormous sigh, laughed an odd little laugh, and stood up. "Let's split what's left of the coffee."

All the clouds were gone now and the full moon lit the wilderness as if it were day. The boys sat and watched the black and silver woods. Daniel poked at the fire. Seth munched on the bag of nuts and raisins, then passed them to Daniel.

Seth began chuckling to himself.

"What's the matter?" Daniel asked.

"You solved the mystery and you don't even know it."

"I did?"

"We've got proof he lasted at least one winter."

"We do?"

"We found him in the cave, right? He only went there in the summer, to watch people, right? He could never get there in the winter. The ice up there would make it impossible. He ran away in the fall. The only time he could possibly have gotten back there was the summer after the first winter."

Daniel smiled. It *was* true.

But the solution to the mystery seemed insignificant now. They had found the truth, but the facts were meaningless to them. Only the boy mattered.

"I want to go back," Daniel said. "I want to spend tomorrow night with the bones."

Seth's heart sank. "Oh, Daniel, I don't want to; I can't." Seth understood why Daniel wanted to return, or at least he had some idea, but he was afraid.

"I'm going. I've got to. Just once. I'm not going to try to talk you into it, but I'd like for you to come with me. Don't decide for sure just now. Sleep on it. You can decide tomorrow."

Then Daniel added, "Speaking of sleep, let's get some. The sun's about to come up."

Both boys climbed inside their bags, and in what seemed like seconds Seth could hear Daniel's deep, even breathing. Seth blew out the candle and zipped his bag. He tossed and turned. He couldn't sleep. Maybe it was the coffee or the decision he had to make or maybe it was all he had just heard.

He propped himself up on one elbow and looked at Daniel through the darkness. Slowly Seth was beginning to understand something about his friend, something about the bones, about loneliness. And part of his understanding was knowing he would never quite understand, at least not the way Daniel understood, not with the fury and pain Daniel felt. But just now Daniel had opened the door into his past, if only just a little, and allowed Seth to look in. Seth was grateful for that.

He lay back. He knew now that he and Daniel were like brothers, but he also knew, for the first time, that like all brothers, they were the same and different, together and alone.

Despite their closeness they were both terribly alone.

9

There was an awkward silence between the two boys over breakfast the next morning. Neither Seth nor Daniel wanted to resume last night's discussion, but it still weighed heavily on their minds, so instead of talking about it, they didn't talk at all.

Finally Daniel said, "How's your leg?"

"Okay. Stiff, but it'll be okay."

"You should probably take it easy this morning, don't you think?"

"I thought I'd just hang around here or something. What are you going to do?"

"Maybe I'll fish down the brook toward home, get us enough for today."

"Daniel, I don't want to go back."

"Let's not talk about it now. At lunch, let's decide at lunch." Daniel wanted Seth to come with him. In fact, he doubted he could make it alone, but he was determined not to force Seth to go.

"Maybe we could just go over there this afternoon, come back in time for supper, not spend the night," Seth suggested.

"No, I want to spend the night up there or not go at all."

"Why? Why do we have to do that?"

"It just has to be that way. We'll talk later. I'm going fishing."

Daniel gathered his gear together and headed down Lost Boy Brook. Something was drawing him toward that pool in the brook where he and his father had first fished together five years before.

When he reached the pool, it was as if he had walked backward into his own past. Everything there was as it had been, the deep pool, the green swirling water, the gravel bar where they had cooked lunch.

Daniel's thoughts wandered back to that other time. He could see an eight-year-old boy standing on the gravel bar with a strange man, a man the boy would come to know as his father. He could see the boy stealing glances at the man's face, wondering who he was, what they were doing here together.

The man helped the boy up onto the big rock that jutted out into the stream, and the boy walked carefully, fearfully, along the spine of the rock toward the stream. The man helped him down into a small bowl in the rock, a seat hollowed out by centuries of high spring water. Daniel watched the boy as he sat at the edge of the stream looking at the rushing water. The boy was smiling; so was Daniel.

Then the boy turned to the man and the man was gone. The boy was alone and crying.

Daniel was puzzled. That was not what had happened. It had been a good day, just as he had described it to Seth. Why then had his memory tricked him and made it seem bad? His good feelings rushed away; he felt alone, like the little boy by the brook, like the boy on the mountain. The old fury rose in his throat. He tried to choke it back, but it was no use. Then Daniel heard himself speaking aloud, the words wrenched out of him.

"I'm alone. I'll always be—just like that kid. I'll always be an orphan. It's too late for me too."

Daniel stepped up onto the rock and settled himself into the seat. He still fit. He leaned back and felt the coolness of the stone through his shirt. Daniel had only slept a few hours last night; he was tired, worn out. He felt like crying, but he was too sad and angry to cry. He closed his eyes and listened to the brook; then he fell asleep.

In a dream Daniel saw himself standing at the edge of a flat, open field. The field was filled with people, old people, young people. Each person stood an arm's length away from those around him. Everyone was reaching out, clawing at the air, calling, straining to touch another, but they could not move; their feet were stuck, rooted, where they stood. The people reached, they strained, but they never touched. Slowly, here and there, a person sunk into the earth and disappeared. Slowly another rose to take his place.

Daniel's eyes wandered through the people. He saw their faces filled with pain, saw how, although they spent their lives trying, they never touched each other.

Then Daniel's eyes moved toward a road that passed beside the field. There was someone standing at the edge of the road, his arms folded across his chest, his face motionless. Somehow Daniel knew it was the boy from the mountain; he was watching the people in the field.

Daniel's eyes came close to the boy, and as they did, the boy's face changed into Daniel's face. For a moment Daniel watched himself standing motionless, cold as a stone, his arms folded across his chest.

Then Daniel heard himself crying out, "*No! No! I am* not *you!*" As Daniel shouted, the face changed back into the boy's face.

Quickly Daniel turned his eyes to the people again. There was his grandfather, who had died three years ago. There was Mr. Bateau and Seth. Everyone he had ever known was there, all the people from his foster homes, the family he had run away from. Everyone was straining, reaching out to one another.

Then Daniel's eyes found what they had been looking for; they found his parents. His parents, like the others, stood facing each other, an arm's length apart. They too reached out; they too could not touch, and their faces were fearful, their hands clawed the air.

Daniel could see himself standing beside his parents. Suddenly all motion stopped. Everyone in the field stood still and stared at Daniel as if they were waiting for something.

Daniel felt an old fear rush through him. Then, slowly, it passed and he saw his arms unfold. He felt his feet root themselves in the earth. He saw his arms and hands begin flowing back and forth like slow fish through water. He saw his body begin to sway. Then Daniel couldn't see himself anymore. All he could see now were the others. When that happened, everyone in the field began moving again, but now, even though they still could not touch each other, they all began to sway just like Daniel. And Daniel could see that everyone was smiling.

As Daniel's body moved with the others, as his hands reached out, he realized he was one of them. They were all there together.

Then the field full of people was gone and all he could hear was the rush of the brook. He opened his eyes. He could feel the coolness of the stone through his shirt.

There was a chickadee sitting on a branch above him, its head cocked quizzically to the side, staring quietly down at him. Slowly, carefully, Daniel reached into his pocket in search of bread crumbs. He took the slight handful he found and gathered them together in his palm. Then he laid his open hand gently on his thigh. Almost immediately the chickadee fluttered down and landed on the toe of Daniel's boot. The bird hopped boldly along his leg and perched on his knee. It hesitated, then hopped directly onto his hand. Daniel could feel the small talons dent his flesh; he could feel the bird's cold feet against his skin.

The chickadee finished the crumbs and for a time stood calmly in Daniel's open hand staring up into the boy's face, then it flew away. Daniel left his hand open on his thigh. For a long time he sat awake and motionless, his eyes wide and unblinking, the way one does after a long and restful sleep.

Usually Daniel had trouble understanding his dreams, but this one seemed easy. He knew now that he was not alone in his loneliness. He was an orphan and there was no way he could change the past or erase those early years. But he wasn't the only one who was lonely. Everyone else was too. He knew Seth was lonely. He had seen him reaching out. And there was Mr. Bateau, who lived alone, without his wife, in that big, empty farmhouse. Daniel knew now why he came every morning, winter and summer, down the road to Daniel's house to gossip and visit. He understood now why his parents took each other in their arms. But mostly what Daniel knew now was what it meant to join the people in the field.

The distance was always there; it always would be. And Daniel realized that for him, bridging that distance would be more difficult than for most people. But he also knew now that to quit trying, to give up reaching across the loneliness, to stand on the road like the boy, arms folded, hands closed, separated from the others, to stand and watch and not reach out, was to die.

Finally he stood up and headed back to camp. He had forgotten entirely that he'd come to fish.

10

When Daniel reached camp, Seth was gone. The fire was down to coals and a large pot of rice stood simmering on a hot stone. Daniel built up the fire a little and put some water on to boil. Then he propped himself up against the lean-to and stared blankly through the woods.

"Hi," Seth said. "Look at these."

Seth had a pail full of blackberries in his hand.

"Good," Daniel said. "We need a little fruit or

something, especially since I didn't get any trout."

"How come?"

A sheepish grin warmed Daniel's face. "Well, I didn't even fish, never got to it."

"What've you been doing all morning?"

"Ah, well, you wouldn't . . . yes . . . yes, you would. But you better sit down. It's going to take awhile, and it's weird, man, it's really weird."

Daniel told Seth everything he had seen in his dream, and as he talked, he felt a feeling rush through him he had never felt before. It was as if he were a bird, a hawk, who had lived his entire life in a cage and then, suddenly, one day the door was opened and the hawk flew out, away, into the free air, higher and higher, until he caught the wind and soared in great circles over the mountains. And as he soared, he cried, fierce, wild cries of sheer joy in the broad and open sky.

Daniel finished his story and the two of them sat for a time in silence. Then Seth said, "I've made my decision."

Daniel cut him off short. "If you don't want to go it's okay with me; I won't go either."

"I'll go."

"Really?"

"Really. It's important to you."

"You sure?"

"I'm sure. I've already cooked the rice for the trip. Besides, I'd like to look at that spear again. I was too scared to look the first time."

The boys ate lunch, packed enough gear for the overnight trip, including water for tea, and headed for the mountain. They retraced the route they had taken through the storm.

They passed the charred ruins of the spruce tree that had exploded into flames in front of them the night before. They could see where it had begun to set the forest floor afire, but the hard rain had quenched the flames before they could spread. Then they were standing again on the summit of the mountain looking down on the world.

They descended to the ledge twenty feet below and found the lost flashlight lying in the opening to the cave. They entered the cave immediately and crawled back to where the bones lay. All the terror they had felt the day before was gone. They were not afraid.

"Let's bury him. We could cover him up with stones," Daniel suggested.

"And let's give him his spear," Seth added.

Seth crawled out of the cave and found the crude weapon lying on the ledge. He examined it carefully, trying to imagine what it must have been like in the boy's hand.

"I wish we could take this back with us," Seth said.

"I wish we could too, but it's not ours. Let's tuck it in here along his side."

The boys began covering the skeleton with stones. Carefully, gently, they mounded rocks over the bones until the bones disappeared completely, never to be seen again.

With the burial complete, Seth and Daniel settled themselves outside the cave and built a small fire from the twigs and sticks they found lying here and there along the ledge. They ate a spare meal of plain rice and unsweetened tea. As the sun slipped down behind the mountains far to the west on the other side of Lake Champlain, deep purples and reds spread across the sky. Then it was dark.

They unrolled their sleeping bags and climbed in. They watched the fire die to coals, heard an owl calling in the night, far below them. They saw the lights of Daniel's house glowing in the darkness. They slept.

When Seth woke the next morning, Daniel's sleeping bag was empty. Seth found Daniel sitting crosslegged on the edge of the ledge, staring down on his farm.

Daniel had gotten up before the sun. He had watched the sun climb over the mountain, heard the ravens croaking in the dawn. He had seen his parents go to the barn to do chores, heard his mother calling the cows in out of the night pasture, seen the cows amble back to pasture, seen his parents return to the house for breakfast. He had heard the morning sounds of a farm, a home—his farm, his home.

"What are you doin', Daniel?"

"Just sittin'."

Daniel stood up. He turned to Seth, stretched, and said, "*Hey, man, let's go home!*"

"*All right!*"

The boys gathered their gear. Then they returned to the cave opening and stoned it up: they filled it with rubble, disguised it so that no one would ever find that place again.

By the time they got back to camp, they were famished, but they were also so eager to get home that they ate only the leftover cold rice and the remains of the sunflower seeds and raisins.

"Should we take the camp apart?" Daniel asked.

"Let's leave it. I think we'll be back. Besides, maybe somebody else would like to use it. It would make a good deer camp."

As the boys cleaned and packed their gear, Daniel began pacing nervously in front of the lean-to.

"I've got to tell you," Daniel said.

"Tell me what?"

"I stole a bone from the boy."

Daniel reached into his pocket and held out a small bone from the boy's hand.

"God, Daniel, how could you do that!" Seth began to laugh. He reached into his pocket and held out another small bone from the boy's hand.

"Why, you . . ."

"What should we do with them?" Seth asked. "Are we going to tell?"

"No, I don't want to," Daniel said. "Let's hide them. When we get home we can find a safe place for them."

The boys mounted their packs and stood for a moment looking at the empty camp.

"There's only one more thing," Seth said.

"What's that?"

"Remember that night before we went to the mountain? Remember that scream? What was that?"

"I don't know. Maybe it was the ghost."

"Come on, Daniel, you know there's no ghost up here. I think it was the panther."

"The what!"

"The panther. I think there's still a panther up here."

"Are you kidding me? Let's get out of here! A panther! Come on!"

Seth laughed out loud.

The boys headed down the brook toward home.

11

They left the cool woods and stepped out across the newly plowed field behind Daniel's barn.

They dumped their packs on Daniel's porch and stepped in.

"Welcome home!" Daniel's mother said.

Mr. Bateau was there.

"Da babies is back! How was it? How you be?"

"Good!" Seth said. "May I use your phone?"

"I've already called. We saw you coming up through the pasture. They should be here any minute."

As she spoke, Seth's family pickup truck pulled into the drive.

"How was fishing?" Seth's father asked.

"Fishing!" Daniel exclaimed. "We're so sick of eating trout, we never want to see another one as long as we live!"

"Come on, now."

"He's not kidding," Seth added. "There's a beaver pond up there so thick with trout you can walk across the water on their backs."

"Dat a lot a trout." Mr. Bateau hesitated, then said, "Did you find da bones?"

"What bones?" Daniel asked.

"You know what bones."

"Well, if there are any bones up there, we never found them."

"That's right," Seth added. "In fact, we never even looked for them. We climbed to the top of Black Spruce, but there's nothing up there but a big cliff."

"You mean der's not even a cave up der?"

"Nope."

"Come on, Seth, let's go swimming."

The two boys bolted through the screened door and raced each other down the lane toward the pond.

"Well, those two are growing up," Daniel's father said.

"They sure are," Seth's mother agreed.

Mr. Bateau stood in the corner of the kitchen, disturbed and hurt. He *still* believed the story. He *wanted* to believe it. Could the boys be right? Could he have been wrong all these years? He knew everybody thought he was and he had never cared, but now, if the boys were right . . .

Mr. Bateau excused himself and headed out the door. As he stepped onto the porch, his eyes fell on the boys' packs. His heart warmed to their worn and dirty, end-of-the-hike clutter. He knelt down next to them. Mr. Bateau knew these packs were the keepers of memories, and he remembered his own days as a boy in the woods.

Slowly, absentmindedly, his hand ran over the packs. He could see a drinking cup protruding from a side pocket. He drew the cup out and held it. There was a plastic bag in the cup and in the bag a small object. It was a bone.

Mr. Bateau took it out and rubbed it between his fingers. He stood up, looked back through the screen door at the parents and smiled. He bent down to tuck the cup and bone back into the side pocket of the pack. He stood up again, the bone still in his hand. Then, abruptly, he jammed the bone into his own pocket and headed down the lane.

The old man could hear the boys shouting and laughing as he approached the pond.

"Hi, babies! Sounds like you have good times like I say you would."

"Yes, we did," Seth said.

"Oh, by da way, Daniel, I was over to yer mudder and yer fadder's house last night."

"Oh, yeah?"

"Yas, I was. I walk home just after dark too."

"Oh?"

"Yas, I do, and I see yer fire on da mountain."

"You did?"

"Yas, I did. Look like it might be where da cave s'posed ta be." Mr. Bateau watched the boys' faces.

"Nope."

"Wall, I be goin' now."

Mr. Bateau turned to leave, then turned again to the boys and said, "Oh, by da way, here somet'ing I find up der on da porch. Maybe it belong to you?"

He held the bone out to them.

Both boys flushed red. A warm smile spread across Mr. Bateau's face. Then the three of them laughed out loud together.

"You babies bedder keep track a dat. Weren't be so good somebody find it, weren't suppose to."

ABOUT THE AUTHOR

DAVID BUDBILL was born in Ohio. He has been at various times a short-order cook, gardener, farm and woods laborer, carpenter's apprentice, and English teacher.

Mr. Budbill has written several plays and two books of poems, the most recent of which is *The Chain Saw Dance*. Of his most recent book for young readers, *Snowshoe Trek to Otter River*, *Booklist* said, "With clean, simple sentences the author captures the lure of the wilderness and the beauty of the animals in their environment."

David Budbill lives with his wife and children in the mountains of northern Vermont.

Now you can have your favorite Choose Your Own Adventure® Series in a variety of sizes. Along with the popular pocket size, Bantam has introduced the Choose Your Own Adventure® series in a Skylark edition and also in Hardcover.

Now not only do you get to decide on how you want your adventures to end, you also get to decide on what size you'd like to collect them in.

SKYLARK EDITIONS

☐	15238	The Circus #1 E. Packard	$1.95
☐	15207	The Haunted House #2 R. A. Montgomery	$1.95
☐	15208	Sunken Treasure #3 E. Packard	$1.95
☐	15233	Your Very Own Robot #4 R. A. Montgomery	$1.95
☐	15308	Gorga, The Space Monster #5 E. Packard	$1.95
☐	15309	The Green Slime #6 S. Saunders	$1.95
☐	15195	Help! You're Shrinking #7 E. Packard	$1.95
☐	15201	Indian Trail #8 R. A. Montgomery	$1.95
☐	15190	Dream Trips #9 E. Packard	$1.95
☐	15191	The Genie In the Bottle #10 J. Razzi	$1.95
☐	15222	The Big Foot Mystery #11 L. Sonberg	$1.95
☐	15223	The Creature From Millers Pond #12 S. Saunders	$1.95
☐	15226	Jungle Safari #13 E. Packard	$1.95
☐	15227	The Search For Champ #14 S. Gilligan	$1.95
☐	15241	Three Wishes #15 S. Gilligan	$1.95
☐	15242	Dragons! #16 J. Razzi	$1.95
☐	15261	Wild Horse Country #17 L. Sonberg	$1.95
☐	15262	Summer Camp #18 J. Gitenstein	$1.95
☐	15270	The Tower of London #19 S. Saunders	$1.95
☐	15271	Trouble In Space #20 J. Woodcock	$1.95
☐	15283	Mona Is Missing #21 S. Gilligan	$1.95
☐	15303	The Evil Wizard #22 A. Packard	$1.95

Prices and availability subject to change without notice.

Buy them at your local bookstore or use this handy coupon for ordering: